Poyser

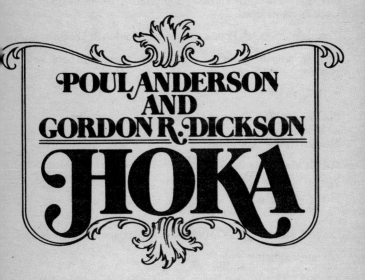

POUL ANDERSON AND GORDON R. DICKSON

HOKA

TOR

A TOM DOHERTY ASSOCIATES BOOK

HOKA!

Copyright © 1983 by Poul Anderson and Gordon R. Dickson

A TOR Book

Published by Tom Doherty Associates
49 West 24 Street
New York, New York 10010

First TOR printing: June 1984
Second printing: October 1985

ISBN: 0-812-53068-3
Can. Ed.: 0-812-53069-1

Cover illustration 1983 © Michael R. Whelan and Walker Brothers

Acknowledgments:

Three of the stories were first published in *The Magazine of Fantasy and Science Fiction*.

"Joy in Mudville," copyright © 1955 The Mercury Press, Inc. Interior illustrations copyright © 1983 by Victoria Poyser

"Undiplomatic Immunity," copyright © 1957 The Mercury Press, Inc. Interior illustrations copyright © 1983 by Nicola Cuti

"Full Pack (Hokas Wild)," copyright © 1957 The Mercury Press, Inc. Interior illustrations copyright © 1983 by Lela Dowling

"The Napoleon Crime," was first published in *Analog Science Fiction/Science Fact* in 1983, and is copyright © 1983 by Poul Anderson and Gordon R. Dickson. Interior illustrations copyright © 1983 by Phil Foglio

Prologue copyright © 1983 by Poul Anderson and Gordon R. Dickson. Afterword copyright © 1983 by Sandra Miesel

Printed in the United States of America

HOKA!

Prologue

From the *Encyclopaedia Galactica*, 11th edition:

TOKA: Brackney's Star III. The sun (NSC 7-190853426) is of type G2, located in Region Deneb, approximately 503 light-years from Sol. . . .The third planet appears Earthlike, to a sufficiently superficial observer. . . .There are three small moons, their League names being Uha, Buha, and Huha. As is customary in the case of inhabited planets, these derive from a major autochthonous language (see NOMEN-CLATURE: Astronomical). It was discovered too late that they mean, respectively, "Fat," "Drunk," and "Sluggish." . . .

At least "Toka" means "Earth." However, indigenous tongues have become little more than historical curiosities, displaced by whatever Terrestrial speech suits the role of the moment. . . .

Two intelligent species evolved, known to-day as the Hokas and the Slissii. The former are quasi–mammalian, the latter reptiloid. . . . Conflict was ineluctable. . . . It terminated after human explorers had come upon the system and the Interbeing League took charge. . . . In effect, the Slissii were bought out. Abandoning their home world *en masse*, they became free wanderers throughout civilization, much to its detriment. (See SLISSII. See also COMPUTER CRIME; CONFIDENCE GAMES; EMBEZZLEMENT; GAMBLING: Crooked; MISREPRESENTATION; POLITICS.)

The ursinoid Hokas generally stayed in place. No nation of theirs refused to accept League tutelage, which of course has had the objective of raising their level of civilization to a point where autonomy and full membership can be granted. Rather, they all agreed with an eagerness which should have warned the Commissioners. . . .

The fact is that the Hokas are the most imaginative race of beings in known space, and doubtless in unknown space too. Any role that strikes their fancy they will play, individually or as a group, to the limits of the preposterous and beyond. This does not imply deficiency of intellect, for they are remarkably quick to learn. It does not even imply that they lose touch with reality; indeed, they have been heard to complain that reality often loses touch with them. It does demonstrate a completely protean personality. Added to that are a physical strength and energy astonishing in such comparatively small bodies. Thus, in the course of a few short years, the "demon teddy bears," to use a popular phrase for them, have covered their planet with an implausible kaleidoscope of harlequin societies describable only by some such metaphor as the foregoing. . . .

Joy
in
Mudville

"Pla-a-a-ay *ball!*"

The long cry echoed through the park as Alexander Jones, plenipotentiary of the Interbeing League to the planet Toka, came through the bleacher entrance. Out on the field the pitcher wound up in a furry whirl of arms and legs and let go. Somehow the batter managed to shift his toothpick, grip the bat, and make ready while the ball was streaking at him. There was a clean crisp *smack* and the ball disappeared. The batter selected a fresh toothpick, stuck it in his mouth, jammed his hands in his pockets, and started a leisurely stroll around the diamond.

Alexander Jones was not watching this. He had heard the crack of the bat and seen the ball vanish; but following that there had been only a vague impression of something that roared by him and smashed into the bench above in a shower of splinters. As a former Interstellar Survey man, Alex was *ex officio* a reservist in the Solar Guard, and the promptness and decisiveness with which he hit the dirt now would have brought tears of fond pride to the eyes of his superior officers had they been there to see it.

However, they were not, and after holding his position for several seconds, Alex lifted a cautious head. Nobody else was up to bat; it looked safe to rise. He dusted himself off while glancing over the field.

It was spotted with small round forms, tubby, golden-furred, ursine-faced, the Hoka natives of the planet Toka. They were all in uniform, the outfit of long red underwear, shortsleeved shirts, loose abbreviated trousers, and peaked caps which had been traditional for baseball since it was invented back on Earth. Even if most of the races throughout the known Galaxy which now played the game were not even remotely human, they all wore some variation of the costume. Alexander Jones often wondered if his kind might not, in the long run, go down in history less as the originators of space travel and the present leaders of the Interbeing League than as the creators of baseball.

Mighty Casey, the planet's star batter, had completed his home run—or home saunter—and returned to the benches. Lefty was warming up before he tried himself against The Babe. Professor, the intellectual outfielder, was at his post, keeping one eye on the diamond

Poyser

while the other studied a biography of the legendary George Herman Ruth. Beyond the bleachers, the high tile roofs of Mixumaxu lifted into a sunny sky. The Teddies were practicing, the day was warm, the lark on the wing, the snail on the thorn.

Putzy, the manager of the team, trotted worriedly up to Alex. He had been called something like Wishtu before the craze reached his planet; but the Hokas, perhaps the most adaptable race in the universe, the most enthusiastic innovators, had taken over names, language—everything!—from their human idols. Though of course they tended to be too literal-minded . . .

"Ya all right?" he demanded. He had carefully cultivated hoarseness into his squeaky voice. "Ya didn't get a concussion or nuttin'?"

"I don't think so," answered Alex a little shakily. "What happened?"

"Ah, it wuz just mighty Casey," said Putzy. "We allus try a new pitcher out on him. Shows him he's gotta woik when he's up wit' duh Teddies."

"Er—yes," said Alex, mopping his brow. "He isn't going to hit any more this way, is he?"

"He knocks dat kind every time," said Putzy with pardonable smugness.

"*Every* time?" retorted Alex maliciously. "Did you ever hear the original poem of 'Casey At the Bat'?"

Putzy leaped forward, clapped a furry hand to Alex's mouth, and warned in a shaking

Poyser

whisper: "Don't never say dat! Geez, boss, ya don't know what duh sound of dat pome does to Casey. He ain't never got over dat day in Mudville!"

Alex winced. He might have known it. The Hoka mind was about as *sui generis* as a mind can get: quick, intelligent, eager, but so imaginative that it could hardly distinguish between fact and fiction and rarely bothered. Remembering other facets of Hoka-assimilated Earth culture—the Wild West, the Space Patrol, Sherlock Holmes, the Spanish Main, *la Légion Étrangère*—Alex might have known that the one who had adopted the role of mighty Casey would get so hypnotized by it as to start believing the ballad had happened to him personally.

"Never mind," he said. "I came over to get you. The Sarennians just arrived at the spaceport and their manager's due at my office in half an hour. I want you there to meet him."

"Okay," said Putzy, sticking an enormous cigar into his mouth. Alex shuddered as he lit up; tobacco grown on Toka gets strong enough to walk. They strolled out together, the pudgy little Hoka barely reaching the waist of the lean young human. Alex's runabout was waiting; it swung them above the walled city toward the flashy new skyscraper of the League Mission.

Seen from above, the town was a curious blend of the ancient and the ultramodern. As a technologically backward race, the Hokas were supposed to be introduced gradually to

Galactic civilization; until they had developed so far, they were to be gently guarded from harming themselves or being harmed by any of the more advanced peoples. Alex, as League plenipotentiary, had the job of guide and guardian. It paid well and was quite a distinction; but he sometimes wondered if it wasn't making him old before his time. If the Hokas were just a little less individualistic and unpredictable—

The runabout set itself down on a landing flange of the skyscraper and Alex led the way inside. Ella, his native secretary, nodded at him from an electrowriter. There was a cigaret in her lipsticked mouth, but the effect of her tight blouse was somewhat spoiled for him by the fact that Hokas have twice the lactational equipment of humans. She was competent, but her last job had been with Mixumaxu's leading Private Eye.

Entering the inner office with Putzy, Alex flopped into a chair and put his feet on the desk. "Sit down," he invited. "Now look, before the Sarennian manager comes, I want to have a serious talk with you. It's about financing the team."

"We're doing okay," said Putzy, chewing on his cigar.

' 'Yes," said Alex grimly. "I know all about that. Your arrangement with these self-appointed outlaws in the so-called Sherwood Forest."

"It's fair enough," said Putzy. "Dey all get free passes."

17

"Nevertheless," said Alex after gulping for air, "things have got to be put on a more regular basis. Earth Headquarters likes the idea of you . . . people playing ball, it's a good way to get you accustomed to meeting other races, but *I'm* responsible for your accounts. Now I have a plan which is a little irregular, but I do have discretionary powers." He reached for some papers. "As you know, there are valuable uranium deposits on this planet which are being held in trust for your people; they're being robotmined, and the proceeds have been going into the general planetary development fund. But there are enough other sources of income for that, so I've decided to divert the uranium mines to the Teddies' use. That will give you an income out of which to pay for necessities"—He paused and frowned. "—and that does *not* include toothpicks for Casey!"

"But he's gotta have toot'picks!" cried the manager, shocked. "How kin he waggle a toot'pick wit'out—"

"He can buy his own," said Alex sternly. "Salaries are paid to the team, you know. The same goes for that bookworm outfielder of yours, Professor—let him pay for his own books if he must read while he plays."

"Okay, okay. But we gotta have a likker fund. Duh boys gotta have deir snort."

Alex gave in on that. The fieriness of the Hoka distillation and the capacity of its creators were a Galactic legend. "All right. Sign here, Putzy. Under the law, native property has to be in native hands, so this gives you title to those mines, with the right to receive income from them and dispose of it as you see fit. Sometime next week I'll show you how to keep books."

The manager scrawled his name as Ella stuck her head in the door. She never would use the office annunciator. "A monster to see you, chief," she said in a loud whisper.

"Ask him to wait a minute, will you?" said Alex. He turned to Putzy. "Now look, please be as polite as you can when the Sarennian comes in. I don't want any trouble."

"What's duh lowdown on dem, anyway?" inquired Putzy. "All I know is we play 'em here next mont' for duh Sector pennant."

"They—well, I don't know." Alex coughed. "Just between us, I don't like them much. It isn't their appearance, of course; I've been friends with weirder beings than they are. It's something in their culture, something ruthless. . . . They're highly civilized, full members of the League and so on, but it's all that the rest of the planets can do to restrain their expansionism. By hook or by crook, they want to take over the leadership." He brightened. "Oh, well, we're only going to play ball with them."

"*Only?*" cried Putzy, aghast. "What's so only about it? Man, dis is for duh Sector pennant. Dis ain't no bush-league braggle. Dis is a crooshul serious!"

Alex shrugged. "All right, so it is." But he could sympathize with his charges. The Hokas

19

had come far and fast in a mere ten years. It would mean a lot to them to win Sector championship.

The Galactic Series necessarily operated under some rather special rules. In a civilization embracing thousands of stars and still expanding, one year just wasn't enough to settle a tournament. The Series had been going on for more than two centuries now. On the planets local teams contended in the sub-series for regional championships; regions fought it out for continental victories, and continents settled the planetary supremacy. Then there were whole systems, and series between systems, all going on simultaneously . . . Alex's brain reeled at the thought.

Extrapolating present expansion of the League frontiers, sociologists estimated that the play-off for the Galactic Pennant would occur in about 500 years. It looked very much as if the Toka Teddies might be in the running then. In one short decade, their energy and enthusiasm had made them ready to play Sarenn for the Sector pennant. The sector embraced a good thousand stars, but Toka had by-passed most of these by defeating previously established multistellar champions.

"If we lose," said Putzy gloomily, "back to duh bush leagues for anudder ten-twen'y years, and mebbe we'll never get a chanst at duh big game." He cheered up. "Ah, who's worrying? Casey ain't been struck out yet, and Lefty got a coive pitch dat's outta dis univoise."

Alex pressed a button and spoke into the

20

annunciator. "Send the gentlebeing in, Ella."
He rose politely; after all, Ush Karuza, manager of the Sarenn Snakes, *was* a sort of ambassador.

The monster squished in. He stood well over two meters high, on long, clawed legs; half a dozen ropy tentacles ending in strong boneless fingers circled his darkly gleaming body under the ridged, blubbery-faced head. Bulging eyes regarded Alex with a cold, speculative stare, but he bowed courteously enough. "Your sservant, ssir," he murmured in tolerably good English.

"Welcome . . . ah . . . Mr. Karuza," said Alex. "May I introduce Putzy Ballswatter, the manager of the Teddies? Won't you sit down?"

Putzy rose and the two beings nodded distantly at each other. Ush Karuza sniffed and unfolded a trapeze-like arrangement he was carrying. When he had draped himself over this, he lay waiting.

"Well," said Alex, swinging into the little speech he had prepared, "I'm sure you two will get along famously—"

Putzy, who had been staring at Ush Karuza, muttered something to himself.

"Did you say something, Putzy?" asked Alex.

"Nuts!" said Putzy.

"Hiss!" hissed the Sarennian.

"Well, as I was saying," continued Alex hurriedly, "you'll get along famously as you ready yourselves for the big contest—"

Putzy seemed on the verge of speaking again.

"—in your *separate* training camps," went

21

on Alex loudly, "at *good* distances from each other—" Under the rules, a team playing off its own world had to have a month's training on the other planet to accustom itself to the new conditions. There was also a handicapping system so complicated that no human brain could master it.

Alex knew what the trouble was this time. It was something he had kept carefully to himself since first learning that the Teddies were to play the Snakes. The fact was that the Sarrennians bore a slight but unfortunate resemblance to the Slissii, the reptile race which had been the Hokas' chief rival for control of Toka from time immemorial till men arrived to help out; and the fur on the little manager's neck had risen visibly at the mere sight of his opposite number.

What was worse, Ush Karuza seemed to be experiencing a like reaction toward Putzy. Even as Alex watched, the tentacled monster produced a small bottle which he opened and wafted gently before his nose like a disdainful dandy of the Louis Quinze period on Earth. For a second, Alex merely blinked, and then a whiff from the bottle reached his own nostrils. He gagged.

Putzy's sensitive nose was wrinkling too. Ush Karuza came as close to smirking as a being with fangs in its mouth could.

"Ah ... merely a little butyl mercaptan, ssirss," he hissed. "Our atmosphere containss a ssimilar compound. It iss nessessary to our

23

metabolissm. Quite harmless to man and Hoka."

"Um ... ugh ... ah?" said Alex brightly. Out of the corner of his eye he saw Putzy grind out his dead cigar in the ashtray and dig another one twice the size out of his baggy uniform shirt. He fired it up. Butyl mercaptan sallied forth to meet and mingle with blue noisome clouds of smoke.

"Ah sssso!" mumbled Karuza furiously and began to waft his bottle more energetically.

Puff! Puff! Puff! went Putzy.

"Gentlebeings, gentlebeings, please!" wheezed Alex, taking the heavy paperweight away from the Hoka.

Venomously hissing, Ush Karuza was uncorking a second bottle while Putzy crammed more cigars into his mouth.

Things were off to a fine start.

Alexander Jones came staggering home to his official residence that night in a mood to be comforted by his beautiful blonde wife, Tanni. But the house was empty, she having taken the children for a few days to the Hoka Bermuda for its annual sack by pirates (a notable social event on Toka), and dinner was served by the Admirable Crichton with his usual nerve-wracking ostentation. It was only afterward, sitting alone in the study with a Scotch and soda, that Alex's ganglia stopped vibrating.

The study was a comfortable book-lined room with a cheerful fire, and when he had slipped into a dressing gown and placed himself before the desk, Alex realized that privacy was just what he needed. He pressed the door-lock button, opened a secret drawer, and got out a sheaf of papers.

Let not the finger of scorn be pointed at Alexander Jones. The most amiable, conscientious, thoroughly normal young men still have their hidden vices; perhaps these outlets are what keep them on their orbits, and surely Alex had more troubles than most who shoulder the Earthman's burden. What the universe needs is more candor, more tolerance and understanding of human weakness. The truth is that Alexander Jones was a poet.

Like most great creative artists, he was frustrated by the paradoxes of public taste. As a Solar Guardsman, he had achieved immortality by his poetic gifts. It was he who had oringated the limerick about the spaceman and girl in free fall, as well as the Ballad of the Transparent Spacesuits, and these shall live forever. Yet they were merely the sparks of his careless youth and he now winced to recall them. His spirit was with the Avantist Revival; his idols had never been known outside of a select clique: Rimbaud, Baudelaire, cummings, Eliot, Cogswell. From time to time the interstellar mails carried manuscripts signed J. Alexander to the offices of *microcosm: the minuscule magazine.* So far, they had also carried the manuscripts back. But a shoulderer of the Earthman's burden is not easily discouraged.

Alex took a long drink, placed stylus to paper, and began writing:

the circumambient snake surrounds the palpitating tarry fever-dream of uncertain distortions and Siva screams and mutters unheard vacillations: now? then?
Perhaps later, it is hot today.—

The visio set interrupted him with a buzz. He swore and pressed the *Accept* button. The features of a rather woozy-looking Hoka appeared on the screen.

"Hi-yah, bosh," said the apparition.

"Putzy!" cried Alex. "You're drunk!"

"I am not," Putzy replied indignantly, momentarily reeling out of screen range. "Shober as a judge," he said, reappearing. "Coupla liters ish all I had. Wouldn't make a pup drunk. It's dis yer stuff Ush Karuza smokes when he's shelebratin'. Dese Sarennians don' drink. Dey just smokes uh stuff. Makes me kinda light-headed—smellin' it—" Putzy went over backwards.

Climbing back into view, he said with heavy gravity: "I called y'up t' tell ya shumfin. You said be nice to Karuza, di'n' ya?"

"Yes," said Alex, a dreadful premonition seizing him.

"Thash what I thought ya said. Well, listen. Like yuh said, we wen' out for li'l drink. Had li'l talk, like yuh said we should. We got t' talkin' shop, shee, an' I tol' him 'bout dose uranium mine rights. Right away he wan'ed

26

ta bet me some salt mines on Sarenn against 'em. So I did."

"You did?" yelped Alex.

"Sure I did. Signed duh papers an' all. Di'n' ya say be nice to him? But listen—" Putzy beckoned mysteriously and Alex leaned forward, shaking. Putzy went on in a whisper. "Here's duh t'ing. Not on'y has has I made him happy, but we got us some salt mines."

"How come?" moaned Alex.

"Because!" said Putzy strongly, driving his point home with a stubby finger jabbed into the screen before him. "Because he don' know it yet, but duh Teddies is gonna win."

"Is that so?" barked Alex.

"Sure, ah' yuh know why?"

Alex shook his head numbly. "No, why?"

"Because," said Putzy triumphantly, "duh Snakes is gonna lose."

He beamed. "Jush t'ought ya'd like to know, bosh. So long."

"Hey!" screamed Alex. "Come back here!"

He was too late. The screen was blank.

"Oh, *no!*" he gasped. "Not this!"

For a wild instant, his only thought was of *quotation at the waterfront*. It had been shaping up so nicely! Wouldn't he ever get a chance to write something really significant?

Then he settled back to realities and wished he hadn't.

Tottering to his office the next morning after a sleepless night, he took an athetrine tablet and called the Mission library to send up Volume GAK-GAR of *Basic Interstellar Law.* When he received it, he turned to the section on gambling between beings from different planets. He had to find out if the bet Putzy had made with Karuza could be legally collected or not. The legislation in question turned out to be full of such witty statements as, "The above shall apply to all cases covered by Smith *vs.* Xptui except in such cases as are covered by Sections XCI through CXXIII inclusive"—each of these with its own quota of exceptions and references. After two hours, he was still no closer to an answer.

He sighed, sent Ella out for more coffee, and was just settling down to a fresh assault on the problem when there was a sort of swirl in the air before him and a semi-humanoid specimen with an enormous bald head topping a spindly little body materialized in his visitors' chair.

"Greetings, youth!" boomed the newcomer. "My visualization of the cosmic all implies that you are surprised. Do not be so. Be advised that I am Nicor of Rishana, who is to umpire the forthcoming contest between Toka and Sarenn."

Alex recovered from his astonishment. The Rishanans, the most intellectual race in the known Galaxy, were almost legends. They could be lured from their home only by a problem impossible for lesser races to solve. Such was any game governed by the 27 huge volumes of the Interstellar Baseball Association rules; as a result, Rishanans invariably officiated in the Series as umpires.

Otherwise they ignored the rest of the Galaxy and were ignored by it. Undoubtedly they had a lot on the ball—for instance, whatever tiny machine or inborn psionic ability permitted them to project themselves through space at will; but since nobody really misses the brains he doesn't have, the rest of the League had never fallen prey to any sort of inferiority complex. Indeed, most beings felt rather sorry for the poor dwarfs. Since the Rishanans felt rather sorry for the poor morons, everybody was happy.

Inspiration came to Alex. "May I ask you a question, sir?" he begged.

"Of course you may ask a question," snapped Nicor. "Any ego may ask a question. What you really wish to know is whether I will answer the question." He paused and looked uncertain. "Or have you already asked me the question? Time is a variable, you know."

"No, I didn't know," said Alex politely.

"Yes, indeed," thundered the voice of that incredible ancient being. "As determined by Sonrak's hypothesis. But come, come, youth—the question."

"Oh, er, yes." Alex pointed to the law book. "I'm having a little trouble with a small point here. Just a—heh! heh!—a theoretical question, you know, sir. If a Hoka bet a Sarennian some Tokan land, and lost, could the—er—say the Sarennian collect?"

"Certainly," snapped Nicor. "That is, he would collect by respective substitute."

"I beg your pardon?"

"You need not apologize for inferior mentality. In effect, the Hokas, being wards of the League, would be protected; but as plenipotentiary and responsible individual, *you* would have to pay the winner an equivalent amount."

"What?" cried Alex as the assessed valuation of the uranium mines—a fourteen-digit figure—reeled before him.

He heard the explanation through a blur. The extreme libertarians who had drawn up the League Constitution had protected ordinary citizens right and left but deliberately placed high officials on a limb. In this case, a judgment in equity would send him to the Sarennian salt mines for—oh, in view of the new longevity techniques, about fifty years, turning his wages over to Ush Karuza. The working conditions were not too bad unless one happened to have a distaste for the odor of the mercaptans.

—"Well, well, enough of this pleasant but unprofitable chit-chat, youth," finished Nicor. "Let us be off to the ball game."

"What game?" asked Alex weakly. "The pennant game isn't for another month."

"Tut-tut," reproved Nicor. "Don't interrupt. I am, of course, both forgiving and gracious. Perhaps you think an intellectual like myself has no sense of humor. So many beings fall into the misapprehension. Certainly I have a sense of humor. Of course, it is more subtle than yours; and naturally I am not amused by the crude horseplay of lesser intelligences. In fact," went on Nicor, his brow darkening, "that is the main trouble with beings of small development. They do not take the cosmic all seriously enough. No dignity, youth, no dignity."

"But wait a minute—" broke in Alex.

"Don't interrupt! As an intelligence of the quaternary class, you cannot possibly make an interruption of sufficient importance to interfere with a statement emanating from an intelligence of my class. As I was saying ... Dignity. Dignity! That is what is so painfully lacking in the younger races." A thundercloud gathered on his face. "When I think of the presumption of those few rash individuals who have dared to question my—MY!—decisions upon the baseball field—But I am sure your charges will be guilty of no such indiscretion."

Alex rocked in his chair. If there was any sport the Hokas loved with a pure and undying love, it was umpire-baiting.

"As for your quaint belief that this is not the day of the game," continued Nicor, "I could hardly expect you to know. You irresponsible children never know. When I was your age, I used to have to get up every morning and figure time as a variable to fourteen decimal places before I could start my day's calculations. We didn't have Sonraks in those days to help us. The trouble with you present youths is that you have it too easy. Surely you do not think I would put myself in the ridiculous position of having to realign my-self for thirty days in the future? Naturally, I devoted only one point eight percent of my reasoning power to this business of establishing my spatio-temporal coordinates, but it is inconceivable that I should fail. No, no, rest assured that this is the day of the game."

Alex pointed a mute finger at the chronopiece on the wall. Nicor whirled and stared at it.

"What?" he roared with a volume that shook the office. "Am I to be given the lie by a mechanical? Am I to be outfaced by a planet? Am I to be maladjusted by a cosmic integral of the square root of minus one over log log tangent X, theta R squared over N dx from zero to infinity? Blast Sonrak! Damn the misplaced decimal point! Time is *not* a variable!"

And with an explosion that rocked the room, he vanished.

Now, it seemed, everything depended on the Teddies winning the game. Alex visited the Hoka ball park and tried to make Putzy institute more rigorous training. The Hokan idea of practice was to let Casey swat a few wild ones while the basemen and fielders sat down, puffing cigars, tilting jugs to their lips, and chatting lightly of this and that. To Alex's protests that the Snakes were bound to get some hits when they came up to bat, Putzy retorted that Lefty would fan them or, failing that, fielders with the speed of the Professor would easily tag them out. Alex gave up.

He made an excuse to drop in on the Sarennian training camp. The visitors were good, no denying that: their main advantage was their terrific tentacle spread, handy for nabbing flying balls; and when the pitcher was winding up, you couldn't see what kind of pitch was coming among all those arms, or even what arm it was coming from. But they lacked the Hoka swiftness and hitting power. Alex—who had spent long hours under a hypnoteacher cramming himself with baseball lore—decided that one set of advantages just about offset the other, so that there would be no handicapping.

Ush Karuza looked positively gloating under his superficial good manners, and Alex began to get suspicious. Considering the ambitions of Sarenn, there was probably more at stake than the pennant and a bet. Returning to his office, the man consulted the Service roster and found that a Sarennian was now at the top of the list of those waiting for ambassadorial vacancies and, if Toka's plenipotentiary were removed, would probably get the job. Sarenn being fairly close to the Tokan sun while Earth was far away, it wouldn't take long for the new chief to gain complete control of the planet for his people without attracting too much attention at Headquarters.

And a plenipotentiary sent to the salt mines would naturally not retain his position.

Alex looked hollowly into space. He didn't even have Tanni to comfort him; she had messaged an intention to stay on a while in Bermuda and he agreed, not wishing to torment her with worry which might turn out to be needless. His carefully guided planet was headed for tyrannous foreign rule; he was headed for the same; *microcosm* had just returned *Greeks En Brochette*. . . .

There is an old saying that, "The optimist declares this is the best of all possible worlds; the pessimist is afraid he's right." Alex agreed.

The big day dawned bright and clear and hot. Since early morning, a colorful throng of Hokas had been flocking into the ball park. They had come not only from Mixumaxu and its neighboring city-states, but reflected the varied impact of human culture on their entire planet. A booted and spurred cowboy sat next to a top-hatted Victorian gentleman; a knight in armor clanked past a tubby Space Patrolman; a sashed character with a skull and crossbones on his cocked hat grumbled saltily, "Scupper my mizzenmast!" as he tripped on his cutlass. One part of the stands was reserved for Sarennian spectators, a silent and impassive mass of tentacles.

As Alex walked across the field to his official seat in the Hoka dugout, he scowled. The substitutes were all present and accounted for, but where was the regular team?

"Hot dogs, pop cawn, soda pop!" bawled a vendor in the stands above. "Getcha pop here, folks. Can't kill duh umpire wit'out a pop bottle!"

Alex's worried eyes traveled across the dusty ground to the center of the infield. Nicor of Rishana was already there, leaning on the bookcase containing the 27 volumes of rules. There was a grim look on his face which might have been caused by thoughts of Sonrak, and a slightly withdrawn expression in his eyes as he mentally scanned the field from all necessary points of view. This psionic ability had enabled the number of umpires to be reduced to one, even as the easy exhaustion of some races had forced changes in the rules governing substitutions.

"Where's our team?" muttered Alex. "They're late already."

The buzz from the bleachers became a chant. "We want the Teddies. We want the Teddies. We want the Teddies."

Then there was a ragged cheer as the famous nine came into sight—not from the locker room, but from the main gate. Even at that distance, Alex saw how they staggered. Leading the way Ush Karuza, looking smug and supporting Putzy, who was singing something about somebody called Adeline. Alex broke into a cold sweat.

Putzy lurched up to him while the rest of the team was calling cheery greetings to their friends in the stands and forcing autographed balls on them. "Hi-ya," burbled the Hoka manager, collapsing into Alex's arms. "I gotta tell ya shumfin. We got dese Sarennians all wrong. Good ol' Ush, he's all right. Ya know what he done? He took us all out dis mornin' an' stood us to duh bigges' dinner in town. All duh steak an' French fries we could eat. Whoops!" He lost his grip and sat down

suddenly. "T'ink I'll take li'l nap." His beady eyes closed.

Alex glared at the Snake manager. "Is this your idea of fair play?" he asked. "Drugging our team. Umpire!"

Nicor flickered in mid-air and appeared beside them. "What is it, youth?"

"This—" Alex pointed shakily at Ush Karuza. "This *gentlebeing* took our men out and drugged them with that stuff he smokes."

"My dear ssir!" protested the monster. "It iss merely a mild sstimulant that we Ssarennianss ssmoke for pleasure. I am not accountable if it affectss our little friendss."

Alex opened his mouth indignantly. "Down, youth!" snapped Nicor. "There is nothing in the rules covering pre-game festivities." He returned to midfield.

Another Sarennian pushed foward a great wheeled tank. "Ice cream," announced Ush Karuza grandly. "Help yoursselfss, my friendss!" As the Hokas threw themselves on it with besotted cries of glee, he pulled a book out of his pouch and gave it to the Professor. "And for you," he added, "a brand-new biography of Tyruss Cobb, sspecially prepared by the Ssarennian Sstate Department."

"Oh, boy!" The small, bespectacled Hoka sat down and began reading it at once. Ush Karuza oozed off with every appearance of satisfaction. Alex buried his face in his hands.

Nicor of Rishana spoke into his wrist microphone, and his voice boomed over the park: "Come, youths! My visualization demands that you now play ball!"

The spectators cheered. The band, somewhat confused, broke into *Auld Lang Syne*. The Toka Teddies wobbled out onto the field. Putzy sat up and muttered something about not feeling so good.

The Snakes, as visitors, were first up to bat. Their star hitter, Shimpur Sumis, wrapped his tentacles around his club and waved it gleefully. Lefty, the Teddy pitcher, found his way to the mound and began turning around to get his position. He kept on turning.

"Play ball, youth!" thundered the umpire. Shimpur Sumis yawned.

It seemed to infuriate Lefty. He sent his ball spinning in faster than Alex could follow. Either because he wasn't quite himself, or because he hadn't allowed for the greater reach of Sarennian tentacles, Shimpur Sumis connected with a solid hit. The ball smacked into left field. The monster dropped his bat and galumphed toward first base.

"Grab it, Professor!" screamed Alex.

The intellectual outfielder was too immersed in his new book to notice. The ball shot past him. His fans howled, "Wake up, ya bum! Grab dat ball!"

Shimpur Sumis rounded second.

A Hoka near Alex, clad in doublet and hose and feathered cap, leaped up, fitted an arrow to his longbow, and let fly. The Professor yelled as it pinked him, glared around, saw the ball, and loped after it. By a miracle, he got it back to the catcher just as Sumis went by third. The Sarennian retreated, grinning smugly.

The next one stepped up to bat. Lefty sent a whizzer past him. The ball smacked into the catcher's mitt.

"Ball one!" cried Nicor.

"Whaddaya mean, ball one?" squeaked Lefty, spinning around in a rage. "Dat wuz a strike if I ever seen one."

"A strike," said Nicor, glowering, "must pass between waist and shoulders."

"Yeah, but he ain't got any waist *or* any shoulders," protested Lefty.

"Hmmm, yes, so I see." Nicor pulled one of the fat volumes out of the bookcase beside him and consulted it. Then he took forth a transit and sighted on the batter. The crowd rumbled impatiently.

"The equivalent median line," said Nicor at last, "yields the incontrovertible result that the missile so injudiciously aimed was, indeed, ball one."

Alex shuddered. Putzy turned green under his fur.

The next ball met a hard-swinging bat. Again it zoomed by the immersed Professor. Again the archer fired. This time the Professor was ready. He plucked the arrow out of the air as it neared him and continued reading. Both Sarennians loped home. Their rooters set up a football-style cheer:

Hiss, hiss, hiss!
Who iss better than thiss?
Squirmy worm, destiny's germ—
TEAM!!!

The next Sarennian went out on a pop fly just behind third. The one after that made it to first. But Lefty, even when pitching on hope and instinct, was not a hurler to be despised. The fifth Sarennian up to bat barely got a piece of the ball and both he and the Snake on base were put out in a wobbly double play.

The Teddies came to bat. They were uniformly ineffective with the single exception of mighty Casey, who, as Putzy was too sick to tell him not to, tried to fulfill a longstanding ambition to lay down a bunt, but only succeeded in bunting the ball over the left field fence. Score one run for the Teddies.

The next four innings were a rout. The regular Teddy team got even sicker and had to be taken out, and against the substitutes, the Sarennians made blissful scores. At the end of the first half of the fifth inning, the board read seven to one in favor of the Snakes.

By the second half of the fifth, the original team members were weak but recovered, and ready to take the field again with blood in their eyes. Casey was first up, and with a valiant return to his usual nonchalance, he put his hands in his pockets and sauntered toward the plate, a toothpick in his mouth and scorn in his eye. He whipped into his batting stance just as the Sarennian pitcher let go. There was a blur, a crack, and he was strolling off along the baseline, nodding graciously to his fans.

But for him it had been a poor and a weak

hit. The Sarennian left fielder reached forth an interminable tentacle and nabbed it as it came smoking along the ground. He whirled and shot it back toward first base. Casey saw it coming and broke into a panting run. He thundered into first together with the ball.

"Out!" said Nicor, appearing at the bag.

"Out???" screamed Casey, skidding to a stop and coming back. "I wuz in dere ahead o' duh ball wit' enough time fer a nap."

"I say *out*," ruled Nicor. "Do not dispute with a superbrain—Time! Don't mention that word *time* to me!"

"Why, ya blind, bloody, concrete-skulled superbrain!"

Pop bottles began to fly from the stands, bursting to fragments in the air as the small robot-controlled anti-aircraft guns mounted on the right field fence went into action. Nicor ignored the bombardment and settled the discussion by flickering back into position behind the pitcher's mound.

The game continued. The Teddies were still a little weak and uncertain. The Hoka following Casey was caught out at shortstop and the next Hoka sent a high fly into right field where it was easily taken for the put out.

The Snakes came up to bat in the first half of the sixth inning. Lefty, turned white-hot with determination, retired the opposing side without gain by three straight strikeouts. The Hokas took over at the plate and the first six men up scored two men and loaded the bases.

The score stood at seven to three with Casey yet to bat, and the Snakes called time out.

"What is the occasion, youth?" demanded Nicor of Ush Karuza.

The Sarennian smirked. "I find I musst invoke one of the handicapping ruless, ssir," he answered. "Article XLIII, Ssection 3, Paragraph 22-b. In effect, it iss that a certain gass iss necessary to our player'ss metabolissm. It being a mercaptan, completely non-toxic in small dosess ass you know, we may ssimply releasse it without sslowing the game down by wearing masskss and handicapping the Hokass."

"There are psychosomatic effects," objected Nicor. "I refer to the nauseous stench involved."

"I do not believe the ruless ssay anything about such side issuess," answered Karuza smugly.

Nicor went back to the books. At last he nodded. "I fear you are right," he added sadly. "But in the name of sportsmanship—"

Ush Karuza turned purple with rage and swelled up alarmingly. "Ssssir! How dare you!" he hissed. "Article CCXXXII, Amendment Number 546, paragraph 3-a, explissitly sstatess that Ssarennianss are incapable of the conssept of Ssportssmanship and sspessifically exemptss them from observing it."

"Oh." Nicor looked crestfallen. He checked. "True," he said bitterly.

Alex felt ill already. This looked like the end.

A great generator was wheeled into an upwind position on the field. It began to fume. Alex caught a whiff and felt his stomach rise in revolt. There could only be a few parts per million in the air, but it was enough!

"Oof!" groaned Putzy beside him. "Lemme outta here."

"You stay," said Alex desperately, grabbing him. "Play up, play up, and play the game!"

Nicor turned a delicate green. "My visualization of the cosmic all suggests I am going to be sick," he muttered.

Putzy opened a box of cigars and passed them around to his team. "Dis may help ya fer a little while," he said. "Now get in dere and fight!" Tears rose in his eyes. "Me aged grandmudder is sitting at home, boys, old and sick, laying dere amongst her roses and lavender waiting for yuh to bring home duh pennant. It'll kill duh sweet old lady if ya lose—"

"Ah, shaddap!" said his grandmother, leaning out of her place in the stands beside him and stuffing her knitting in his mouth.

Alex fumed away on his own cigaret, trying to drown the smell that curled around him. There must be *some* way to escape those salt mines!

With the mercaptan turning his stomach upside down on top of the effects of the drug, Casey still batted in the man on third on a sacrifice fly. The Hoka following him struck out. Retired, the Teddies lurched out onto the field and took another pasting. The score climbed against them—six Sarenn runs in the

seventh, seven in the eighth, with the brief one-two-three interlude of the Teddies at bat hardly noticeable in the Snakes' slugging festival. When the Hokas came up again in the top of the eighth, they were trailing twenty to four.

Alex chewed his fingernails. There *must* be an answer to this! There must be some counter-irritant, something which would get the Hokas back to the careless energy and childlike enthusiasm which served them so well. . . . Counter-agents! The idea flared in his head.

He snatched at the water boy's arm. "Bring us something to drink!" he commanded. The little ursinoid sped away, to return with a slopping bucket which Alex knew very well did not contain water.

"Time out!" he yelled. "The Hokas request time out."

"What for, youth?" asked Nicor faintly.

"They need alcohol to protect themselves against the effects of the Sarennian gas. It's okay by the rule books, I'm sure."

Nicor brightened a little. "It does protect?" he inquired. "Then, youth, you may bring me some too."

Ush Karuza jittered about in a rage while the Teddies gathered weakly around the bucket and dipped their noses into it. Even by Hoka standards, they got it down fast. Nicor scowled at his complimentary beaker, sipped, winced, and gasped. *"This* is necessary to them?" he cried. "I have seen halogen breathers, I have seen energy eaters, I have seen drinkers of molten lead, but here is the race that shall rule the sevagram!"

Casey lifted his dripping black snout. "Urp," he said. "Gotta toot'pick?"

"Play ball!" hollered Ush Karuza wrathfully.

The Babe waved casually at Putzy. "We'll get 'em," he said confidently, and connected with the first pitch for a clean single to left. The Professor came up with his book in one hand, stuck it under his arm just long enough to belt one out of the park, and walked home with his nose back in his book.

"Geez!" he muttered reverently. "Dat Cobb could sure play *ball*!"

Lefty stepped up to bat with an evil gleam in his eye. The Sarennian star pitcher launched a ferocious fast ball across the middle. Lefty let it go by. "Ooooof!" said the catcher.

"Strike one," said Nicor.

Time out to replace one catcher.

There was no second strike. Lefty bounced the next pitch off the right field wall for a stand-up triple.

Casey sneered and sauntered out to the plate. Grabbing the end of the Sarennian catcher's fourth tentacle, he began picking his teeth with it.

"Halt! Stop! Foul!" shrieked Karuza. "He *bit* my player!"

Some of Alex's hard-won baseball knowledge came to his aid. "Article XLI, Section 5, Paragraph 17-a: 'Players may take such nourishment as is required during the game,'" he flung back.

47

"But not off *my* players!" wailed Karuza.

Nicor weaved over to his books and consulted them. "I am afraid I can find nothing forbidding cannibalism," he announced. "It must never have occurred to the commission. Tsk, tsk."

The pitcher let fly. Casey set his bat end-on on the plate and jumped up to balance on top of it. "Strike one!" called Nicor.

"Nope," said Casey owlishly. "Yuh mean ball one, ump. Duh ball went under m' waist. Under m'feet, in fack!"

"So it did," agreed Nicor imperturbably. "Ball one!"

"The ruless—" sputtered Ush Karuza.

"Nothing in the rules against balancing on top of a bat, youth." Nicor scratched his bulging head. "I do believe the commission will have to call a special meeting after this game."

The Sarennian pitcher wound up again. As the ball zoomed toward him, Casey swung the mightiest swing in Toka's history. The Snakes' second baseman saw the ball screaming at him and dropped to the ground in terror. A bolder monster in the outfield raised his glove and caught it. Or perhaps one should say it caught him—he was lifted off the ground, described a beautiful arc, and landed three meters away. The ball went merrily on to cave in a section of the fence beyond.

Casey, who had been spinning on one heel unable to stop, came to a halt and staggered around the bases. He had plenty of time, be-

cause the Sarennians had to dig the ball out from between two planks.

Time out while the Snakes replaced one unconscious outfielder and one second baseman with a bad case of the shakes.

The rest of the Hokas followed the example of their star players and sailed twice completely through their lineup before being retired with a score of 19 to the Snakes' 20 at the end of the eighth. The crowd, including Alex, was going wild.

Shimpur Sumis came up to bat with a haughty look suggesting that he alone could settle the matter. Lefty, who was higher than a kite, threw him a ball so fast that it exploded on being struck. Nicor consulted his library for the rule on exploding balls, found none, and called it a strike ... though he admitted that his visualization was not very complete today. Sumis' abused tentacles could not handle the bat well enough to keep him from being struck out.

Ush Karuza snarled and went over to the mercaptan generator and opened the valves wide. A thick, nearly visible stream of vapor rolled across the field to envelop the Hoka pitcher.

Lefty was too drunk to care. He sent off his famous curve. Then he gaped at it. So did the Snake batter. So did Alex. No—the ball couldn't possibly be where it was!

It landed in the catcher's mitt. "Strike one!" announced Nicor.

The next pitch was even more unbelievable

than the last. It defied all known natural laws and went in a sine curve. "Strike two!"

The batter flailed wildly the third time. Alex distinctly saw the club go through the ball, but nothing happened.

"Strike three!" said Nicor. "Youth, you are now external to the n-dimensional sociological hypersphere!"

"Huh?" asked Putzy.

"He means, 'You're out,'" translated Alex happily.

"Foul!" bawled Ush Karuza. "They're using black magic."

"There is nothing in the rules against magic," said Nicor.

"I just t'row a damn good coive, dat's all," said Lefty belligerently.

The next Sarennian fared no better. By that time Alex had figured out the situation. "The thick stream of mercaptan vapor has a refractive index appreciably different from air," he told Putzy. "No wonder it produces optical illusions. Hoist by their own petard!"

Putzy seemed dubious. "If dat least means what I t'ink it means," he said, "you shouldn't oughtta say it in front of me grandmudder."

The Teddies came to take their turn at bat. It was the last half of the ninth inning. The score stood at 19–20 with the Teddies trailing. The batting order at that moment stood: first The Babe, then the Professor, then Lefty, and then Casey. The Sarennians looked grim, but the Hokas in the stands, who had resorted to their potent pocket flasks while the team was getting their liquor from the water boy, were wildly jubilant. As The Babe picked up his bat and strode to the plate they began a cheer which finally died away to an awful silence as the whole crowd held its breath.

The Sarennian pitcher was clearly determined to let no hits be gotten off him. He wound up and let fly.

From the stands rose a mighty groan of horror, interspersed with shrill hoots of glee from the Sarennian section. For the stream of mercaptan vapor was still flowing past the pitcher *and all three balls wove a daisy chain past the plate!*

"Strike three!" cried Nicor. "Out!"

Sadly, The Babe came back. The stands were in an uproar. It looked as if open battle might break out between the Hoka and Sarennian fans. Alex cringed on his bench.

The Professor went up to the plate. The ball looped crazily by him. "Strike one!"

A long moan of agony went up from the Hokas.

"Strike two!"

The Professor braced himself. There was a wild, almost berserk gleam in his spectacles. The Sarennian pitcher writhed and twirled his tentacles with contemptuous confidence. The ball shot forward.

The Professor threw himself and his bat to meet it.

There was a tiny *tick*. The ball popped out of the vapor fog and trickled along the ground toward third base. There were only a few

seconds of time before it was caught, but that was all the Professor's famous legs needed. There was a whiz, a blur, an explosion of dust, and the Hoka was safe at first.

The tying run was on, and there were two outs left to bring it home.

Lefty took his time selecting his bat. He swung it heavily a few times to test the balance and then slowly stalked up to the plate. The pitcher wound up. He threw. The stands groaned.

"Strike one!" thundered Nicor in a voice of doom.

The Sarennian catcher strolled out to return the ball to the pitcher. They conferred for a few seconds.

With the batter back in position, the pitcher wound up again. The ball snapped out of his mass of tentacles, flickered, and appeared in the catcher's mitt.

"Strike two!"

"Casey," said Putzy in a shaking tone, "get ready, boy."

Alex turned to look at the Teddies' mainstay. To his surprise, the little batter seemed cool and calm. "Relax, Putzy," Casey said. "It's in duh bag. All I gotta do is knock us bot' home."

"But dose pitches!" said Putzy.

"Lissen!" said Casey with some heat. "Lissen, ya don't t'ink I ever bodders to watch d' pitcher, do yuh? All I pays attention to is duh ball from duh time it gets to about two meters away from me. And duh ball gotta be straight den, or duh ump calls it a foul. Dey can't fool me none."

Slowly, hope began to dawn on Putzy's furry face. He was even smiling as Nicor called "Strike three!" and Lefty returned glumly from the plate.

Casey got to his feet and began his customary nonchalant stroll toward the batter's box. At first the crowd merely gaped at him in astonishment; but then, drawing courage from his apparent confidence, they raised a swelling cheer that rocked the stands. He doffed his cap and kissed his hand to the fans, waved, rubbed his hands in the dirt and took up his stance. Alex saw, through a vision blurred by tenseness, that the Sarennian pitcher was already losing heart at sight of this overweening opponent.

"Time out!" screamed Ush Karuza.

For a moment the park was held in agonized silence. Then a mounting growl like that of a Boomeringian sea-bear disturbed at its meal commenced and grew.

"For what reason, youth?" saked Nicor.

"Article XXXVI, Ssection 8, Paragraph 19-k," said Ush Karuza defiantly. "Any manager may encourage hiss team by verbal meanss."

Nicor checked. "Correct," he said. "You may proceed."

There was a scurry from the Sarennian dugout and a public address system was wheeled onto the field and its microphone set up before a small tape player. As the stands waited silently to see what this new move might portend, Ush Karuza switched it on. There was a hissing noise as the machine warmed up.

At the plate, Casey smiled indulgently.

And then the hissing stopped and a voice boomed over the park. It was not a Sarennian voice, but human; and the first words it uttered wiped the smile from Casey's lips and fell on the field like the hand of doom. For the voice was reciting, and the first words were:

It looked extremely rocky for the Mudville nine that day:
The score stood two to four with but one inning left to play.
So when Cooney died at second . . .

"Oh, no!" wailed Putzy. "It's *it!*"

"What's it?" choked Alex.

"Dat pome—'*Casey At duh Bat*'—oooh, lookit poor Casey now—" The manager pointed a trembling finger at the Teddies' last hope, who was shaking with unbearable sobs as he stood at the plate.

"I protest!" screamed Alex, leaping from the bench and running wildly out to where Nicor stood.

"You have no right to protest," snapped the umpire, "You are merely a spectator."

"Den I pertest!" roared Putzy, skidding to a halt beside Alex. "Turn dat t'ing off!"

At the plate, Casey was melting down in his own tears as the tape swung into the fifth stanza.

Then from the gladdened multitude went up a joyous yell.
It rumbled in the mountaintops, it rattled in the dell,
It struck upon the hillside and rebounded on the flat.
For Casey, mighty Casey, was advancing to the bat

Casey was flat on the ground now, making feeble pawing motions as if he would dig his grave where he lay, crawl in, and die.

"Your protest is out of order," said Nicor.

Ush Karuza oozed oily sympathy. "I am afraid your batter iss not feeling well," he muttered.

. . . And when the writing pitcher ground his ball into his hip,
Defiance gleamed in Casey's eye, a sneer curled Casey's lip. . . .

Abandoning the umpire, Putzy ran to his collapsed star and tried to lift him from the ground. "Fer cripessake, Casey," he pleaded. "Stan' up. Just get us one little hit. Dat's all I ask."

"I can't," choked Casey. "Muh heart ain't in it no more. Dey trusted me in Mudville and I let 'em down."

The stillness over the park was broken only by his sobs and the inexorable recorded voice.

> . . . *Close by the sturdy batsman, the ball un-*
> *heeded sped.*
> *"That ain't my style," said Casey. "Strike one!"*
> *the umpire said. . . .*

Like a drowning man, Alex saw his whole life parade by him: Tanni, the children, Earth, Toka. It was not what he wanted. He wanted some way out of this inferno.

No other batter had a chance; the Teddies were too demoralized. But what to do, what to do? Surely he, Alexander Jones, had some means of helping, some talent—He gnawed trembling fingers as the poem tolled its way to its dreadful conclusion.

> . . . *And now the air is shattered with the force*
> *of Casey's blow!*

Damn all poets!

> *Oh, somewhere in this favored land*
> *the sun is shining bright,*
> *The band is playing somewhere and*
> *somewhere hearts are light,*
> *And somewhere men are laughing, and*
> *somewhere children shout,*
> *But there is no joy in Mudville—*

Poetry!

—MIGHTY CASEY HAS STRUCK OUT!

"Yipe!" said Alex.

There was one other outstanding ability which Ensign Alexander Jones had shown in the Guard besides hitting the dirt. And that was that when the occasion arose, he was very quick off the mark when there was something to be run to, or from. Therefore, just as some weeks earlier the promptitude with which he nosedived would have pleased his superiors, so now they would have joyed to see the speed with which he covered the distance between the umpire's post and the public address system. Even the Professor would have been pushed to match his velocity; and the way he stiff-armed the lone Sarennian guarding the recorder was a privilege to observe.

He snatched up the microphone and panted into it. "Go on, boss!" yelled Putzy, unsure what his adored plenipotentiary intended but ready to back him up.

"Pant, pant, pant," boomed Alex over the field.

Ush Karuza ran to stop him. "Hold, youth!" ordered Nicor. "He has a right to use the machine."

"Pant, pant," panted Alex, and began to improvise:

"But hold (pant), what strikes the umpire, what causes him to glare

With fiery (pant, pant) look and awful eye upon
 the pitcher there?
And Casey takes the catcher by the collar with
 his hand;
He hales him to the (pant) umpire and together
 there they stand."

Beside the plate, the Hoka Casey lifted his head in wonder, and wiping the tears from his eyes, stared openmouthed at Alex.

The human had had his dark suspicions about the way Lefty was struck out last time. No chance to prove that, but he could weave it into his revenge.

'I bid you look,' cried Casey, 'I bid you search
 him well.
For such as these our fine fair game they soon
 would sound its knell—!' "

Alex hesitated, looking a trifle confused. "Dat's my plenipotentiary who said dat!" cried Putzy's grandmother; and thus heartened, he proceeded.

"The umpire checks them over and the villains'
 faces fall
When out from each one's pocket he pulls forth
 A HIDDEN BALL!
" 'Oh, shame!' cries out the Mudville crowd.
 The echoes answer, 'Shame!'
'That such a dirty low-down trick should blight
 our Casey's name.

61

The pitcher only faked his throw, the catcher
    faked his catch.
The cowards knew that such as they were never
    Casey's match.' "

"You untentacled mammal!" raged Ush
Karuza. "You sslimeless conformation of boned
flesh!"

Alex had long ago discovered that mankind
rarely reacts to insults couched in nonhuman
terms. It did not offend him at all to be told
that he was slimeless.

The Teddies' Casey was sitting up by the
plate now and beaming. Alex took a deep
breath and went on:

" 'Now take your places once again. Once more!'
    the umpire cried.
'And your next pitches will be fair or else I'll
    have your hide.
Now take your places once again, to places one
    and all!'
And as soon as they were ready, the umpire
    cried, 'Play ball!' "

The Hoka Casey was up on his feet and
clutching his bat. His eyes were riveted on
Alex. And as the last two stanzas came out,
his little form hunched and twisted through
the motions Alex described.

*"And now the pitcher takes his stance, his face
    is black and grim*

*And he starts his furious windup with a fearful
    verve and vim.
And now he rocks back on his heel; and now he
    lets it fly.
The ball comes sizzling forward watched by
    Casey's steely eye.*

*"For Casey does not tremble, mighty Casey
    does not balk,
Though it's clear the ball is high and wide, and
    they aim to make him walk.
He steps forward in the batter's box, his bat's a
    lambent flame.
Crack! Smash! The ball flies o'er the fence—AND
    CASEY WINS THE GAME!"*

The stands were going crazy. Hokas of all
shapes, sizes, and descriptions came pouring
down from their seats to mob and congrat-
ulate—

—Casey, of course.

Who else was responsible for the Mudville
win?

To Hokan taste, it was almost an anticli-
max after the glorious victory of the fictional
Casey when the factual one playfully tapped
a home run over the left field fence and won
the Sector pennant.

In spite of custom, Alexander Jones did not
preside over the wild festivities that night. He
felt he deserved a quiet evening at home, alone
with a tall drink and *quotation at the waterfront.*
Tanni would be coming back soon, and much

as he longed to see her, he knew she would give him no chance to produce something really significant—some poem reflecting the realities of Life.

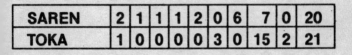

SAREN	2	1	1	1	2	0	6	7	0	20
TOKA	1	0	0	0	0	3	0	15	2	21

Undiplomatic
Immunity

*I was born with a dull, sickening thud. Had I
but known what an aching void yawned before me, I would never have started down that
lonely road.*

"Well—er—" said Alexander Jones, putting
down the sheet of paper. "It's . . . um . . . interesting. But don't you think some of the
phrases are a little, hm, hackneyed?"

"Of course," said the Hoka with the tweed
coat and calabash pipe. He leaned back in his
chair and cocked his feet up on the electrowriter: a meter or so tall, round-bellied,
golden-furred, ursinoid, an outsize teddy bear
with stubby hands and eager button eyes. His
name was W. Shakespeare Marlowe. "Don't
you see, it is precisely by the use of the hackneyed phrase, the integral unit of language
itself, that I create the Myth."

Alex, who was a tall and lanky young human,

sighed. That was what came of letting a Hoka read 20th-century criticism. "But why did you stop there?" he asked.

"I have to leave something to the reader's imagination," pointed out the writer. "That's the quintessence of art. Think how dull and prosaic it would have been if I had gone on to describe the rest of my life."

"Oh," said Alex weakly. "I see."

"Those are the same views intrinsic to my essay, *The Novel As An Art Form*. I have it here—" W. Shakespeare Marlowe produced another sheet from his pocket. "Observe, it says: *'The Novel As An Art Form*, by W. Shakespeare Marlowe. Paragraph. The novel *is* an art form. Period. The end.' Succinct, isn't it?"

"Very," said Alex.

"I knew you'd understand. I call it the new look in writing. Actually, it has its roots in Hemingway. But I refined it to its present form. You see, the trouble with writers has always been that they wrote too much. It cut down their production."

"Cut it down?" asked Alex uncertainly.

"Of course. Look at Twain, Dickens, Melville—a mere few dozen books. Whereas I often write a dozen novels in one day."

"Oh, no!" groaned Alex.

"Quite," said the Hoka, sticking his hands in his pockets and puffing complacently on his pipe.

They were alone in the outer office of the Tokan delegation's suite. A broad window revealed the spectacular towers of League City, spearing into the serene late-afternoon sky of New Zealand, Earth. A webwork of elevated mobilroads knitted the pinnacles together, from the soaring bulk of this official hostel to the immense hall where the Council of the Interbeing League met.

From the adjoining room came subdued squeaks of excitement. Alex wondered what the other Hokas were up to. So far he had kept them out of trouble, but . . .

W. Shakespeare Marlowe, his secretary, was a very mild case, having merely gone overboard for authorship. But the energy, enthusiasm, and literal-mindedness of Alex's charges could lead to their playing any role that struck their fancy with an almost hypnotized solemnity. It was fortunate that the Tokan business stood high on the agenda of the present Council session: the less time on Earth they had, the less chance for some disastrous escapade.

Alex glanced at the wall chrono. He was supposed to meet informally with Commissioner Parr in a few minutes, and had already dressed for the occasion in suitably dignified crimson tunic and green slacks. "We'd better be going, Marlowe," he said. The little Hoka stumped happily out with him.

Two slideways and a dropshaft brought them to a tasteful suite in which cocktails and canapés were laid out. Adalbert Parr, the Chief Cultural Commissioner, received them: a big, portly man with a florid face and wavy gray hair. He bowed stiffly, shook hands, and widened his eyes as Marlowe whipped out a pad and took notes. Then, with regulation heart-iness, he waved at the others present.

"We were only to get acquainted, Plenipo-tentiary Jones," he said. "May I present the chief delegates from three planets in your sector? His Excellency, Representative His Highness Prince Idebar of Worben."

The Worbenites were from a fairly terrestroid planet, a highly civilized race, and Prince Idebar was known as one of the shrewdest diplomats in the Galaxy. He was tall, with sleek black hair, his face aged but still keen and aquiline, his carriage erect; indeed, to be completely human-looking he would only have had to trim his ears and remove his horns and spiked tail. The females of his species were less manlike. "Delighted, sir," he mur-mured.

"No more than I, sir," replied Alex with equal urbanity.

They bowed. Alex jumped back as the horns swept by his nose.

"Ahem!" said Parr. "May I present His Excellency, Tantho the Hairy, leader of the delegation from Porkelans."

This being was two meters high, barrel-shaped, with enormous four-fingered hands at the end of short, muscular arms. He wore only a pocketed belt, but long blue fur cov-ered his body. Two small eyes peered out of a face mostly hair, with just a suggestion of snout. "Most pleased," he rumbled in the offi-cial English of the League.

71

"Her Excellency, Miss Zuleika MacTavish of Bagdadburgh," intoned Parr.

As Her Excellency came into view around the bulk of Tantho, Alex had a sense of being hit with a perfumed blackjack. The Scottish-Arabic colony, founded by a rather puritanical group, had followed the usual law of reaction to interesting extremes. Zuleika MacTavish was tall and willowy, with flowing brown hair and great liquid eyes and a wide soft mouth and ... well, the few wisps of colored translucency making up her native costume gave even an old married man like Alex a slight impulse to throw back his head and howl.

However, plenipotentiaries do not howl, or slaver, at beautiful representatives from neighboring planetary systems. Not if they want to stay on good terms with the Cultural Office of Earth Headquarters and—most particularly—their wives. So Alex goggled and sputtered in what he hoped was a suitably diplomatic manner, and scarcely noticed the dark, hawk-faced Colin MacHussein who was introduced as the delegate's special assistant.

"Please sit down, gentlebeings," said Parr. A servant offered a tray of drinks. Alex reached for an interesting-looking green one. Prince Idebar muttered an alarmed *"Garrasht!"* and caught his arm and warned:

"Excuse me, sir. That happens to be made from the jithna leaf of my planet. I believe it is chemically quite similar to poison ivy." Alex shuddered his thanks, and Idebar took the drink himself and sipped with practiced grace.

"Oh, His Highness has no reason to murder *you*," said Zuleika MacTavish acridly. She took a cigaret from her belt pouch and a long holder from her décolletage. Alex came out of a reverie in which he wished he could be—temporarily, of course—a cigaret holder, to hear Parr exclaim:

"Please! We save the, ah, disagreements for the agenda. This is merely a social gathering. My own concern is with Plenipotentiary Jones's planet, Toka, but I thought an exchange of views with his neighbors out in Sector Seven might be . . . enlightening. He is here to see about getting the autochthones upgraded."

Alex nodded. "The Hokas have met the requirements for Class C by establishing a planet-wide peace authority," he said—careful not to add a description of a meeting of teddy bears from nations modeled on the Wild West, Victorian England, the East Roman Empire, King Arthur's realm, and others. "Guiding them is, of course, my task, and I believe they are now ready for Class C." That was mostly a technicality, involving science scholarships for qualified natives, but an essential step on the path to full autonomy and membership in the Interbeing League.

The catch was, there were too many planets in process of becoming civilized, each a complicated special case. The League Council voted on their status, but in practice, of necessity, always followed the recommenda-

tion of the Commissioner. Which meant that
Parr had to be convinced. Alex prayed that
Worben, Porkelans, and Bagdadburgh had no
objections to the upgrading. Quite apart from
the Hokas themselves, it would mean a sub-
stantial raise in salary for him.

However, the little session was uneventful.
The diplomats made polite noises and then
returned happily to throwing courteous venom
at each other. Alex got a distinct impression
that there was trouble between Bagdadburgh
on the one hand and Worben and Porkelans
on the other. It was with some relief that he
finally excused himself.

W. Shakespeare Marlow followed him cheerily down the hall. "I can never thank you
enough for bringing me along," he burbled. "I
have notes for three new novels . . . sensational!
The *haut monde*, wild, dissipated, the orgies
as world-weary, cynical beings flog their jaded
senses with ever new and more fantastic
pleasures—"

"I thought they were rather dull," said Alex,
with regret.

"It is the business of the artist to select and
rearrange his material," said Marlowe firmly.
"How else shall he portray the essence of Life?"

The main door to the Hoka suite opened
before them and Alex trod in. He had left his
delegates alone all day while he went through
some necessary red tape, and had barely noticed that they sent out for some special items.
Now, as he entered the living room, he stopped
dead.

"Yipe!" he said.

Three Hokas sat around a table drinking tea. Two of them had adorned their rotund forms with archaic striped trousers and cut-away coats; top hats lay beside them. The third was completely muffled in a long black coat with its collar turned up, his beady eyes peering out from beneath a black slouch hat. They were being waited on by a fourth in chauffeur's uniform.

"What is this?" cried Alex. "Tharaxu—"

"The name," said one of the Hokas in cutaway, "is now Allenby. Foreign Office, don't y'know. Come join us in a spot of tea."

Alex's gaze roved wildly about the room. He saw numerous books from the hostel's extensive library. The authors were unfamiliar to him—Eric Ambler, E. Phillips Oppenheim, Sax Rohmer—they must be centuries old. The Hokas had apparently dialed for novels about the diplomatic service and—

He clenched his teeth and sat down. "I don't believe I've met the other gentlemen," he said in a hollow voice.

"Forgive me, old chap," said Allenby. "More tea, Bert."

The chauffeur poured.

"Who's Bert?" inquired Alex.

"Our chauffeur, of course," said Allenby. "Foreign Office has 'em, don't y'know." He bowed at the other cutaway. "Heinrichs."

"Heinrichs?"

"Code expert," said Allenby, gazing distantly

at Heinrichs. "One of these efficient German types."

Heinrichs beamed. He had always been near-sighted and worn contact lenses; these he had now discarded for two monocles.

"Code?" choked Alex.

"Naturally," said Allenby. "My dear old chap (more tea, Bert. Thanks), surely you don't imagine we'd dare communicate with the home office except in code?"

"Oh," said Alex. Allenby sipped at his tea. Marlowe took notes. "And . . . er . . . this other gentleman?" said Alex when it became clear that the Hoka in the black hat was not going to be introduced.

Allenby looked around the room, leaned over the table, put a furry hand to his mouth, and whispered: "That's Z."

"Z?"

"Z," breathed Allenby. "You remember Z, of course. The chap who was so useful to us at the time of the Balkan crisis."

"Oh," said Alex.

He was too late. The Hokas were already off on their own path. He could only play along. "Well, gentlemen," he sighed, "you must not forget that this delegation has an important job to do—a *very* important job."

"Hear, hear," cheered Marlowe.

"The future of Toka depends on it," said Alex earnestly. "If we don't get upgraded this time, we can't apply again for twenty years."

"Roight!" said Bert.

"Bert!" said Allenby.

"Sorry, guv'nor," said Bert.

"We have to remember that we are on trial—"

"More tea, Bert," said Allenby.

"Yes, sir."

"On trial, I say. The future of Toka depends on our making a favorable impression. You must remember—"

"Knockout drops, Bert."

" 'Ere you are, sir."

Alex frowned, but was too busy explaining to inquire what was meant. "In most cases," he went on, "there is a delicate situation existing just under the surface of polite intercourse—"

"Let me give you a fresh cup of tea, old bean," said Allenby.

"Thanks," said Alex. "As I was saying, there are conflicts—" He took a swallow from his cup. "There can be situations that—"

The floor came up and hit him.

He struggled back to consciousness to find himself neatly laid out on a couch, and the suite empty. Two hours had passed; it was now 2030 o'clock. He felt like retreaded oatmeal.

After a while he managed to get to his feet, stagger to the bathroom, and gulp down an athetrine tablet. The pains vanished and his head cleared.

"Omigawd!" said Alex. "The Hokas!" He went out the door at full gallop.

Each floor of the hundred-story hostel—this was the 93d—had its own lounge. Alex burst into this room and found its comfortable chairs deserted, its robobar humming softly as it polished glasses . . . no sign of his charges. He was about to dash on, he knew not whither, when a glorious shape undulated through the rear entrance, paused, and sped forward. The soft eyes of Zuleika MacTavish fluttered incredible lashes at him and the soft hands with their luminous nail polish gripped his.

"Oh . . . Plenipotentiary Jones," she whispered. "I was hoping I could find you alone."

"You were?" squeaked Alex.

"Please," she said. "I'm in desperate need of help."

Alex, who had been pawing at the floor in his eagerness to be off, began to paw a little more slowly. Not that the situation wasn't bad, with the Hokas on the loose; but after all, any gentleman who called himself a gentleman—

"Well, er, hruff!" he coughed. "If there's anything I can do—"

Zuleika leaned toward him, still several centimeters removed but slightly indenting his tunic. "It's not for myself, it's for Bagdadburgh," she pleaded. "There's so few of us, and those awful Worbenites and Porkelugians—" Suddenly her eyes were swimming with tears, and Alex put a fatherly arm around her.

"There, there," he began.

A shrill voice exploded behind him. "I say!"

Alex jerked free of the ambassadress and turned to confront the stern gaze of Allenby.

"Oh, er, good evening," he mumbled.

"Beg your pardon, old grapefruit," said the

small Hoka frostily. "Your presence is required at the suite."

"Alex," breathed Zuleika, "I just have to talk with you."

"Yes, yes," said the man. "Later . . . to be sure, later—"

Zuleika gave him a thousand-watt smile through a mist of tears and walked slowly off. Alex stared after her, trying to recall the equations of simple harmonic motion. Allenby tugged at his sleeve. As they left, he found himself blushing, and the more angry he got on that account the more he blushed.

"Well, Allenby," he said gruffly.

"Well," repeated Allenby.

"Charming young lady," said Alex in a frantic tone.

"Yes. I rather imagine you feel like a father toward her."

"Why, of course. How did you know?"

"We," said the Hoka wisely, "know their methods."

"Methods?" asked Alex in bewilderment. "Whose methods?"

"You force me to be blunt, old parsnip," said Allenby. "The methods of beautiful spies. . . . Hist! Not another word till we're back. These walls have ears, don't y'know."

"Oh, no!" groaned Alex as he realized he had been cast in the role of Colonel Blimp.

"Play up, play up, and play the game!" said Allenby, patting him on the arm. "Stiff upper lip. Bite the bullet." With a courteous gesture, he produced a bullet from his cutaway and offered it.

"Play up yourself!" screamed Alex. "Now you listen to me—"

The slideway had borne them around a corner, and they saw Commissioner Parr's ponderous form on the opposite strip. He waved agitatedly at them and stepped onto the motionless central band. "Plenipotentiary Jones!" he barked. "What do you make of this?"

And he thrust under Alex's nose a large, ornate Oriental dagger.

"Found it stuck in my door," went on Parr. "Pinning down a note." He held out the message, and Alex read:

WHERE ARE THE SECRET PAPERS?

"Ulp," said Alex.

"Do you know whose idea of a joke this is?" rumbled Parr. He glared suspiciously at Allenby. "Have you seen this knife before?"

"I?" asked the Hoka. "Can't say I have, old cabbage." He helped himself to a pinch of snuff.

"Well . . . it's odd, to say the very least." Parr bowed stiffly, got back onto the westbound strip, and dwindled down the hall. Alex and Allenby continued east in a chilled silence.

The human found the suite in a state of hideous confusion. Its tables were heaped with paper of all sorts and varieties, and Heinrichs was busily examining these with a magnifying glass. Bert was making tea, Marlowe was writing, and Z sat muttering into his slouch hat.

"*Ach!*" said Heinrichs, looking up. "*Vere vas der hochwohlgeborene Bevollmächtigter Jones?*"

"With," said Allenby in tones of deepest deprecation, "*her.*"

"*Her?*"

"*Her,* herself!"

"Now cut it out!" roared Alex. "Now listen to me! I won't have this—I positively forbid—" Suddenly and belatedly he realized from the happy expressions on the furry faces that he was once more sliding into the character they had determined he should play.

As he stood sputtering, Marlowe looked up and said eagerly: "What do you think of this, Jones? I'm making a new translation of the *Iliad.*"

"You are?" asked Alex blankly.

"Yes, indeed," beamed Marlowe. "I have chosen to represent the timeless spirit of Homer by using the metrical form most characteristic of our age, a rapid, mellifluous—well, hear for yourself." He cleared his throat and read:

> "*I sing of the wrath of Achilles,*
>   *which gave the Achaeans the willies.*
> *Help me tell, O my muse,*
> *how Troy got the goose*
> *and of quarrels which really were dillies.*"

Alex was saved from making noises like a critic by the buzzing of the visiphone.

He pressed the button and Parr's thunderous face popped into the screen. "Plenipotentiary Jones!" he said. "Would you come down to my apartment right away, please?"

Alex nodded and clicked off, wondering what had happened now.

"Z," said Allenby, "attend the Chief."

"Und better you take mine Luger," said Heinrichs, withdrawing a young cannon from his top hat.

"No!" cried Alex. But as he sped out, Z followed relentlessly.

It occurred to the human as he went down the corridor that he could at least get an explanation of what had been going on. "Z," he said firmly, "I want an explanation of what has been going on. In the first place, what was the idea of giving me knockout drops?"

"Policy, sir," said Z.

"Policy?" Alex snapped his mouth shut. Oh, no, he thought, he wasn't going to get into one of those brain-tangling discussions this time. "What about that dagger and note?" he demanded.

"Sir?" asked Z cautiously.

"Do you know anything about that?"

"What can one say?"

Alex stared at him, but he volunteered nothing further. "Well," asked the man finally, "what *can* one say?"

"Exactly," said Z mournfully.

"Exactly *what*, for the love of Saturn?" snarled Alex.

"Exactly nothing."

Alex choked. "All right," he said. "Tell me one thing. Just one thing. What's this all about? What's supposed to be going on?"

"Ah," said Z darkly. "Who can tell?"

"Can't you?"

"Sir!" cried Z reproachfully, drawing himself up. "I'm in the secret service. I never tell."

Before Alex could think of a reply, they were at the Commissioner's suite. Grouped around a table were Parr, Prince Idebar of Worben, Tantho the Hairy of Porkelans, and Zuleika MacTavish of Bagdadburgh. An air of tension prevailed.

"Oh, good evening, Jones," said Parr distantly. "Ah . . . this is one of your delegation?"

"Um, yes," said Alex. "Commissioner, Your Excellencies, Mr. Z."

"How do you do, Mr. Zee?" said Parr.

"One has one's methods," said Z mysteriously.

Parr looked a bit startled, but turned to Alex. "I asked you here because your delegation and Their Excellencies all have accommodations on the 93d floor, and no one else. Possibly we can throw some light on a, ah, very delicate and unfortunate situation. It seems that Their Excellencies have had their suites broken into and stripped of papers."

"Aha!" said Z.

They all stared at the Hoka. "What?" asked Tantho.

"Just aha," said Z. He pulled an Oriental dagger from his sleeve and began idly to clean his fingernails with its tip. Parr's eyes narrowed, but before he could speak, Zuleika flared:

"Can't you see, these, these *gentlebeings* were out to find what they could in my quarters, and just pretended to have their own broken into as well?"

"Your young Excellency," crackled Prince Idebar, "may I point out that a planet must resent slurs on its accredited representatives?"

"Please!" said Parr. "We only wish to get to the bottom of this. I suggest that the Interstellar Bureau of Investigation—"

"No!" snapped Tantho and Zuleika, while Idebar murmured: "I am afraid that that is impossible."

"Ah—" began Z, but Alex hastily clapped a hand over his muzzle and babbled: "I'd better check my own place. I didn't notice any signs of burgling, but . . . I'll let you know—" With a sick grin, he hurried Z out.

"—and furthermore," stormed Alex when he was back in his suite, "breaking into the quarters of Council delegates is a territorial violation. I never saw anything like this! How did you—"

"Aow, naow," said Bert modestly.

"You, Bert?" whispered Alex.

"Of course, old onion," said Allenby proudly. "Bert is an ex-master criminal (now reformed, right, Bert?) and it was jolly old child's play for him, eh, what, what, what?"

"But those locks are finger-sensitive—pick-proof!" said Alex.

86

"Simple, h'it were," said Bert. "H'I took me little h'ax—" He reached inside his uniform with a flourish and brought out an object like a giant jackknife with a hundred blades; from the body he snapped a small but wicked-looking axhead. "—then h'I took me little gouge"—he unfolded something like an icepick—"and me little jimmy, me little bryce and bit—"

Alex turned slightly green. "I see, I see," he groaned. "You needn't go into details."

"H'I picked those locks orl roight. H'I'd like ter see the lock h'I couldn't pick—"

"Bert!" reproved Allenby.

"Roight, guv'nor. Sorry, guv'nor." Bert lapsed into silence.

"—Anyway," said Alex after drawing a deep breath, "breaking into private offices and so forth . . . filling up our rooms with stuff like this—" He grabbed a handful of papers from under Heinrichs' magnifying glass. "What is this, anyhow? Here—

Dear Miss MacTavish: This is to notify you that payment on your account for three black silk negligees, Size 12, and four pairs Upthrust brassieres, 107 cm. large, is now overdue—" Hrump, we won't go into this. Hum." Alex cleared his throat and hastily shuffled the documents. "What's this, a private letter? Don't you know that one of the worst invasions of privacy is to read somebody's else's— um, I see the Worbenites have adopted English as their own international language— *'Dearest Iddykins—'* Good Lord, *Iddykins!*

87

'*Dearest Iddykins, I had a dream last night and I dreamed you were speaking in the chamber of Earth but they had the ventilation turned up for the Chokgins representative. There you were, with nothing but your lightweight underwear on. For eighty years I've begged and prayed you to dress sensibly in your long woollies, you know you get the sniffles so easily, and I've tried to be a good wife to you but the moment you are out of my sight you cast caution to the winds—*'"

Catching sight of the interested Hoka faces ringing him in, Alex broke off and cried wildly: "What do you want with this stuff?"

"Ve must decode," said Heinrichs.

"Ve must?" echoed Alex. "No . . . I mean—these aren't in code, dammit!"

"*Ja*, dey are."

"No, *no*, NO!"

"My dear old artichoke," said Allenby, "with all due respect, who is the code expert here, you or Heinrichs?"

"Heinrichs, of course!" roared Alex. "I mean—no, that's not what I mean. What I mean is—Now don't get me off on *that*! The point is, this is a complete farce. There's nothing going on here"—the door chimed and Alex backed toward it, talking as he went—"that requires daggers in doors, burgling—come in—reading personal papers and so forth—come in, I said—and so on, and now that I have you here I'm going to show you that this business of intriguing is just something you've dreamed up—"

Becoming impatient, he opened the door

manually. Leaning against the jamb, his face shaded by the tartan burnoose, was the silent and faintly sinister Colin MacHussein.

"Oh," said Alex. "What is it?"

To the Hokas' unbounded delight, MacHussein started to lean forward as if to whisper confidentially in his ear. The only problem was that he kept on leaning, further and further, until with a rush he ended face down on the carpet.

"MacHussein!" gasped Alex.

The Bagdadburgian did not reply. But for this seeming rudeness he had a good excuse. It consisted of a headgear the back of which was matted with blood.

Alex spun around and counted his Hokas. They were all present. He sat down and buried his face in his hands.

" 'Ere, sir," said Bert sympathetically. " 'Ave a nice 'ot cup of tea."

"Thank you," said Alex in a weak voice, accepting it. Then, cautiously: "No knockout drops, are there?"

"Aow, no, sir. Cream and sugar, two lumps."

"Thank you," repeated Alex and drank. "It's good."

"Thank *you*, sir. Bucks yer h'up h'in a tight spot, a bit of tea, don't it, sir?"

"Yes," said Alex. "Yes, indeed. When it's been a bad day ever since morning and when a man's been murd—" He leaped as if stung. "WHAT," he screamed, "AM I DOING SITTING HERE AND DRINKING TEA?"

"Thirsty, perhaps?" suggested Marlowe.

Alex slammed down the cup and saucer, shoving aside Z, who was about to search for secret papers. To the plenipotentiary's immense relief, the man was alive: it was the unpleasant but not grave effect of a powerful supersonic stun beam fired at short range.

"The body, of course, will have to be disposed of," said Z.

"No!" Alex began to function again. "Get out—all of you. Go get Parr, get a doctor, but for heaven's sake don't tell anyone what's happened. Get out!"

They got.

Left alone, Alex tried to remember his first-aid training. There wasn't much he could do except leave MacHussein undisturbed. The usual result of supersonic stunning was amnesia covering the past several hours. . . .He grew aware that this fumbling had gotten blood all over his tunic and slacks. Hastily he went to the bathroom, stripped off the clothes, washed his hands, and donned a robe. As he came out, the door chimed again. "Parr," he muttered, and aloud: "Come in."

Zuleika MacTavish sine-waved through, closing the door behind her. Deep, agitated breathing expanded her chest, which was not something Alex would have considered possible had he thought about it dispassionately. "Alex!" she said in a frantic whisper. "There's not a minute to lose. I have to talk to you!"

"Oh—" Alex jittered about. "Well, er, sit down, but—"

"This is no time to sit down." She followed him across the room, completely overlooking the corpse-like MacHussein. "This is the eleventh hour, Alex," she said, cornering him and seizing the lapel of his robe, "I know about you. I know your record. You have your heart in the right place."

"I do?" asked Alex feebly.

"Yes," said Zuleika. "Like me."

"Um . . . to be sure," mumbled Alex.

"You are the only man who can help me," cried Zuleika, throwing herself on his shoulder and bursting into tears.

"There, there," said Alex. He meant to pat her gently on the back, but somehow his hand slipped. "There, there, there." Getting no result from this, he disentangled himself, went to the brandy decanter, and poured out a stiff drink. She accepted it blindly and tossed it off at one gulp.

"It can't be that bad—" Alex was saying, when he was interrupted by a strangled, though ladylike, snort. Zuleika's finely molded face squeezed up, both hands flew to her throat, and she began to stagger around the room making ineffectual noises.

"What is it?" yelped Alex. Smitten with a horrible suspicion, he sniffed at the decanter. It was . . . yes, for his ambassadorial brandy the Hokas had substituted their native liquor, a 180-proof liquid dynamite which—"Omigawd! I'm sorry! Excuse me! 'Ere, 'ave a nice cup of 'ot—No, no, I mean, ice water—"

Zuleika downed it shakily, brushed aside

his babbled apologies, and said with a new and fascinating huskiness in her voice: "No matter. Too much else to do. Prince Idebar and those awful Porkelugians—Goldfarb's Planet—you've got to help me! The whole future of Bagdadburgh depends on it!"

Alex found himself so busy unraveling her explanation that he forgot both MacHussein and the notoriously sudden wallop which Hoka brew delivers. Goldfarb's Planet was a terrestroid world out in Sector Seven; having no aborigines, it was open for colonization, but the award lay with the Council. Bagdadburgh, with a rapidly increasing population (if Zuleika was representative of its womenfolk, thought Alex, he could understand why they had a population problem), needed it badly, and would normally have been granted the title. Porkelans was also asking for it, but the reason was a mystery: their population was static. However, the Bagdadburgian intelligence service had discovered that Prince Idebar of Worben intended to support the Porkelugian claim—and his influence was so great that he was bound to get what he wanted unless he was blocked.

"But what's in it for Worben?" wondered Alex. "I know their present leaders belong to the Expansionist Party and they'd like more territory, but they already have the legal limit of colonies."

"The Porkelugian government is corrupt," said Zuleika fiercely. "Tantho and his associates . . . bribed . . . betraying their own planet. Bribed by dirty Worbenite neodymium."

"Um . . . wait . . . you mean if Porkelans gets Goldfarb's Planet—"

"The Tantho gang would admit Worbenite settlers. In a few years, there'd be so many settlers they could vote for autonomy. But the Goldfarbian government would be a Worbenite puppet. We know it, I tell you. Tantho is selling out his planet for Worbenite neodymium. Would I touch their tainted money? I would not. You would not. But Tantho will. He does. He touches their tainted money every day. I'll bet he's sitting in his suite right now touching Worbenite money."

"But how do you know all this?"

"We got spies," hissed Zuleika. "We found out . . . Tantho an' Idebar got a written agreement about it. Don't trust even each other . . . got a regular contract . . . tainted money." She looked at him with vague, though lovely, brown eyes. "You wouldn't touch Worbenite money, would you?"

"N-no," said Alex. "I guess not. Not if it's tainted."

"Private contrac' . . . would be proof we need to bust rotten con—conshpi—plot. Bust it wide open. Colin s'posed to steal contrac'. Special agent of ours. Where's Colin?" Zuleika peered about in a charming misty fashion. "Will you help me, Alesh?"

"I, well—"

"Oh, thank you, Alesh!" cried Zuleika, staggering a trifle. "Tha's y'r name, isn' nit? Oh, Alesh, hol' onna me, I feel a li'l dizzy—"

The door chimed.

"Hurray for Bagdadburgh!" whooped Zuleika. "Bagdadburgh, my ain planet! Would I stop at anything for Bagdadburgh?" she demanded of the empty air. "No!" she answered with a ringing cry, dramatically seizing the front of her wispy tunic and ripping it across. Then she stumbled over MacHussein, looked down, whitened, screamed, and fell into Alex's arms.

The door opened and Commissioner Parr strode in with several Hokas. He stopped dead.

Alex stared at him, dumbfounded. He could see no reason why the Commissioner should look at him with loathing. Then, glancing at a full-length mirror across the room, he reeled. In its crystal depths he saw a man in a dressing gown clutching a hiccoughing girl with torn tunic while at his feet another man lay weltering in blood and behind him two tables groaned under stolen papers.

"Commissioner!" bawled Alex in tones of anguish. "You don't think—you can't believe—Commissioner!"

"Please, Mr. Jones," said Parr loftily, withdrawing. "Don't paw me."

Alex had been protesting his innocence for a couple of minutes now. The Commissioner did not appear to be convinced. He stood in the middle of the room and stared coldly at Alex while MacHussein lay on the floor and

95

Zuleika lolled in a chair. Even the Hokas were silent.

"But it's not what it looks like!" gibbered Alex.

"Hiccup!" said Zuleika.

"*I* didn't stun this man!" cried Alex. "I sent for you myself—"

"And the representative?" asked Parr scornfully. "I imagine she, too, fell through the door in her present condition?"

"No! She just took a drink, that's all."

"Which you gave her."

"Well, yes, but—"

"Ha!"

"I gave her the wrong thing."

"Indeed you did."

"Whoops!" said Zuleika faintly. "Porkelans, Worben—poke 'em inna nose. Throw'm to the bushcats."

"Now, Mr. Jones," said Parr, "you still have the status of your office and, therefore, diplomatic immunity. My hands are tied. But I shall, of course, make urgent recommendations to my superiors tomorrow to the effect that Toka badly needs a new plenipotentiary and, as the result of—to put it in as kindly a light as possible—your incompetence, the planet is not yet ready for advancement in grade."

If he had been perfectly fair, Alex might have agreed that Parr had a case. But it was *his* job, his reputation, and his Hokas that were at stake. He clutched at a straw. "You don't understand," he said. "I discovered there was an illegal conspiracy between the Worben and Porkelans delegates. Since the IBI can't act against diplomats, I had to use my own status to get the proof."

He flattered himself it was a good speech, but Parr gave him only the thinnest of smiles. "If such proof is forthcoming," said the Commissioner, "naturally I will reconsider. May I see it?"

"I—well—I haven't got all of it yet—"

"I thought not. It is my duty to inform Their Excellencies of the situation, and the aspersions you have cast on them must, of course, be taken into account in judging your case. Good evening, Mr. Jones." Parr bowed and went out.

Alex sat down and grabbed at the decanter. Before he could sort out his whirling thoughts, Marlowe trotted in with the hotel physician.

"Ah," said the doctor cheerily, bending over MacHussein, "a stun beam. Tsk-tsk. But we're feeling much better now, aren't we?" Getting no response, he removed the burnoose and examined the injury.

Marlowe peered over his shoulder. "I am writing a novel about the medical profession," he squeaked. "Heroic, unselfish—"

The doctor reached for his stethoscope. It wasn't there. Z was peering into it for secret papers. "Hey!" said the doctor. Marlowe took busy notes as man and Hoka wrestled for the instrument. Winning the fight, the doctor checked his patient and prepared an athetrine injection. "This'll bring him around," he explained. "He should be all right when he wakes up."

"Aha!" said Z. "When he starts his drugged babbling—"

"Aren't you going to operate?" asked Marlowe, handing the physician a scalpel from his bag.

"For God's sake, no!"

"Not even a little operation?"

"*No*, I said! Get out of my way!"

"You have the soul of an editor," said Marlowe. "Instead of a novel, I think I shall write an exposé."

Somehow the doctor got MacHussein injected, bandaged, and laid out on a couch. He departed muttering.

Alex had recovered his wits enough to give Zuleika a soberpill. They stared grimly at each other.

"Well," said Alex, "I just hope you were right about that contract, and that we can find it. Otherwise—"

The girl nodded. "No less than four of our best secret agents learned of its existence just before I left for Earth," she said. "It'll be here somewhere—the Embassy Building Offices aren't private enough, and naturally it must remain secret to all but a few."

"But why did you—Damn it," protested Alex, "this is serious and I have to think. Will you *please* get another tunic?"

Zuleika looked down and blushed. She was, of course, wearing her Upthrust brassiere, 107 cm. large, but it was made of Sheerglo fabric, which happens to be perfectly transparent. Hastily she went to the closet and borrowed one of Alex's tunics. He was a reasonably athletic young man, but it was still a tight fit around the chest.

"Why did you drag *me* into this?" moaned Alex.

"I had to have someone," she pleaded. "You see, I was getting suspicious of Colin. He has been a secret agent of Bagdadburgh for years, but since we reached Earth I saw him too often talking with Idebar. I turned to you because you, well, you looked so strong and self-reliant and . . . oh, I'm *so* grateful to you—"

"Hrumf!" said Alex. "Never mind. Quite all right."

Zuleika swayed closer. "The whole future of my planet depends on finding that contract," she whispered. "I would do *anything* to get it—to get your help—"

"Now . . . now, wait . . . I've got a wife and . . . and children on Toka and—and—" Alex backed up. His collar felt tight. "Just take it easy."

"After that reception today, Colin disappeared," went on Zuleika. "I got desperate and came here. It was hard to believe anything wrong about him; he's worked with me for years, and always been such a perfect gentleman, though with his looks he could—Never mind." She sighed. "Of course, his being attacked like this proves I was mistaken." She laid her hands on Alex's shoulders and searched his eyes with her own. "But we still need your help."

"And I guess I need yours," agreed the man. "If we can find that contract, it'll clear us, but—"

"I'll be quite frank with you," said Zuleika. "We were going to burgle their apartments, but apparently your Hokas beat us to it, though how you knew even before I told you—" She regarded him worshipfully.

"Oh, well," said Alex with due modesty. "One has a knack—*Hey!*"

Zuleika jumped. This made her quiver. This in turn distracted Alex so much that he could not go on for a few seconds. Then he turned excitedly to the stolen papers. "But the contract must be *here!*" he shouted. "We're saved!"

"Whee!" said Bert, doing a swan dive into the nearest stack.

It took only a few minutes in spite of the Hokas' help. After that there were several more minutes of frantic re-searching. At the end, Hokas and humans regarded each other rather bleakly.

There was no contract. There was not even a protocol.

"I found a treaty on import quotas of rugglepthongs," said Allenby with an air of having done his best.

Colin MacHussein groaned and stirred. Zuleika went to the couch and sat down, laid his head on her breast and stroked his hair. "There, there," she crooned.

MacHussein blinked his eyes open. *"Garrasht!"* he mumbled. "What—oh—" He grew aware of them. "What happened?"

"Does it hurt much?" asked Zuleika softly. "Here, lie back and rest."

"No, I'm all right," said MacHussein crisply. He sat up. "But everything else is wrong. You haven't found that contract, have you?"

"No," said Alex. "What happened to you?"

"I don't know." MacHussein frowned, concentrating. "My memory stops several hours ago. Amnesiac effect, you know. But where did all this litter come from?"

Alex explained. "Apparently the contract isn't in this hotel after all," he finished.

MacHussein shook his head. "It would have to be, for their purposes. Have to be available for reference. But they knew we'd lift it if we could, so they must simply have hidden it better than we realized."

Bert bristled. "They couldn't 'ide nothink from me!"

"Afraid they did. We'll just have to try once more." Alex opened the door and peered out, to meet the unmistakable chilled-steel gaze of an IBI man. Others patrolled the slideways as far as he could see.

"Er...we don't need protection," said Alex weakly.

"No, sir," said the IBI agent. *"You* don't."

Alex closed the door.

"Hist!" said Z, at the window.

"Hist yourself," said Alex bitterly. "We *can't* get to their rooms now."

"There are," said Z, "other methods."

"What other methods?"

"I cannot tell," said Z.

However, he could act, for he opened the window. Alex went over and looked out. A meter below was a flange, some 20 centimeters wide, running around the tower for the benefit of the window-cleaning machines. Beneath, except for other flanges, was a good 400 meters of sky terminating in some very hard-looking pavement.

"Ulp!" said Alex.

"En avant, old turnip," said Allenby with revolting cheerfulness. Carefully he donned his top hat, put a fresh carnation in his buttonhole, stuck a rolled umbrella under one arm, and vaulted out onto the ledge.

MacHussein swallowed. "I'd better stay and hold the fort," he offered.

"No—" Alex gave up. There was no escape for him, unless he wanted the Hokas to go off with no one to control them. But he took some satisfaction in pushing MacHussein to the window. "Miss MacTavish is the one to stay behind."

"Nonsense!" said Zuleika. "I told you I would do anything for my planet."

"Even on a window ledge?" asked Marlowe, interested.

"Even on a window ledge," she declared.

Alex got out into a fresh night wind that nipped his bare shanks but cooled his ears somewhat. Allenby was ahead of him; Bert, happily snapping and unsnapping tools from his instrument, came after; Zuleika, Z, Mac-Hussein, and Marlowe followed.

Under better conditions Alex might have enjoyed the view. The great city sprawled for kilometers around, its arrogant pinnacles reaching for the stars, its roadways a faerie web of lights; far off, under a low moon, he could see the snowy heights of Mount Aorangi. But hugging a slick plastic wall with his heels sticking out over the edge of nothing—

"Naow 'ere, guv'nor," said Bert, "h'is the neatest bit of h'it h'all. See, h'I h'unfold this little drill, turn this little wheel, h'insert the nitro with this little 'ypodermic—clever, eh?" He nudged Alex knowingly in the ribs.

"Yipe!" said Alex.

There was a low wail behind him. Zuleika was shuffling along with her face to the wall. For her, though, this was not very practical.

"Turn me around, somebody!" she begged.

"Right-o," said Allenby gallantly. He reached past Alex and Bert with his umbrella. "Hold on to the end of this and step off the ledge; I'll swing you over to me. We Hokas are quite strong."

Alex assured her of this, and she obeyed. Then she vanished as the handle and the ferrule parted company. "Oh, piffle," said Allenby in an annoyed tone. "I forgot this was also a sword cane. Sorry, old girl."

Just in time, Bert grabbed her hair. This overbalanced Bert, who snatched at Alex. Alex clutched after Allenby, who also toppled but managed to throw his umbrella up for Z. The secret agent got it and went over the brink, dragging MacHussein along. Marlowe got MacHussein by the left foot and hooked his free elbow under the windowsill so he could take notes. Not till he had finished this did he use the really astonishing Hoka strength to draw himself back through the window and then haul in the rest. The most irritating part of it all was that as he pulled in the living rope, he piped forth a deep-sea chanty.

"Not making much progress, are we?" asked Allenby with undiminished good humor. His eye fell on Heinrichs, seated with paper and pencil. "Stop that and come along with us!"

"But I iss decoding!" protested Heinrichs.

"You can decode as we go," said Allenby sternly. He wheeled about and went over the sill again. There was nothing to do but follow him.

This time the path was negotiated without incident. They rounded the corner of the building and saw ahead of them the windows of the Porkelugian and Worbenite suites. The former glowed with light; the latter, beyond them, were dark.

The windows were broad enough so that the whole party could stand looking in. The upper transoms were open, and words drifted out—conversation between Prince Idebar, Tantho the Hairy, and Commissioner Parr, who were sitting about with drinks and cigars.

"—most kind of you, sir, to warn us about those Hokas," said Tantho.

"Oh, just doing my duty," said Parr. "But

I'm sorry I can't legally recover those papers for you until Jones has been fired."

"No matter," said Idebar, waving his tail airily. "I assure you we are not so foolish as to leave confidential documents where any unscrupulous hireling could find them. We have our methods."

This was too much for Z. He whipped out a dagger and tossed it expertly up, through the transom and across the room, to stick quivering in the wall before Tantho's sheepdog nose.

"What's that?" roared Parr, leaping to his feet.

Z pulled down his slouch hat and rubbed his hands. "We too have our methods," he said with a fiendish cackle.

It is disconcerting, to say the least, to be having a private chat on the 93d floor of an official building, and then suddenly to have daggers quivering in the wall and see five teddy bear noses flattened against your windowpane. When one nose is surmounted by a top hat, one by a black slouch, one by a chauffeur's cap, and one by two gleaming monocles, the effect is positively unnerving.

"What kind of place is this, anyway?" stormed Tantho with a not unjustifiable huffiness.

"Spies!" hissed Idebar, gliding forward.

"Spies yourself!" said Zuleika.

"Cut that out!" said Alex raggedly. "We've got to—"

Allenby was already scuttling down the flange to the Worbenite windows. The rest followed. Bert got to work cutting out the livingroom pane. Behind them, Parr looked out, bellowing like a wounded bull. "Thieves! Barbarians! You'll get psychorevision for this, Jones! You—"

"Not so fast, please," squeaked Marlowe, busily taking notes.

"He iss schpeaking in ein zimple double-transposition cipher," decided Heinrichs, looking over Marlowe's shoulder.

"—and naow me little saw," said Bert, "and me little roll of tape, and me little—"

The pane gave way with a crash, and the burglars scrambled through. There was only the vaguest possible illumination from outdoors, but as he fumbled for the switch Alex could see MacHussein's shadowy form atremble. "Sunspots, what a day!" stammered the Bagdadburgian. "I need a drink—" He groped over to a barely visible decanter and put it to his lips and shuddered with relief.

Alex turned on the lights as the outer door opened. An IBI man looked in. Z sent a dagger whisking past him. The IBI man withdrew and Alex scurried about locking all the doors.

Feet thundered in the corridor. "Open up!" bawled Tantho.

Alex groaned. "We've got to find that contract fast," he chattered, staring at the wild disorder left by the previous Hoka visit . . . or visitation. "They'll break in—and for all we know, it's in the Porkelugian suite—"

Allenby glared at an inoffensive chair, broke

off its tail-rest, and ripped the cushion with his sword cane. "Not here," he announced.

"Of course it isn't," said Z. "Don't you know secret documents are always left in plain sight?" His eyes glittered around. "Aha! I've found it!" He snatched a framed paper off the wall. Alex took it with shaking hands and read:

WHEREAS H. H. IDEBAR FANJ HURTHGL HAS SATISFACTORILY COMPLETED THE REQUIREMENTS FOR THE DEGREE OF MASTER OF ARTS IN THE FIELD OF GLOG-SNORGLING, NOW THEREFORE BY AUTHORITY OF THE REGENTS . . .

"It vill haff to be decoded, of course," said Heinrichs.

The door glowed as someone turned a ray-beam on it.

"Too late," said Alex dully.

The door fell, and Parr, Idebar, Tantho, and a dozen grim-faced IBI men rushed through. Alex stared down the muzzles of their Holmans and raised his hands.

"I've got you now, Jones!" raged Parr. "Diplomatic immunity or no, I'm going to have you locked away till—"

"We are not disposed to be malicious, Commissioner," said Idebar with his usual suavity. "Obviously Jones is a public menace, but we see no reason to press charges against the others."

"Aha!" said Z darkly.

"Guilty conscience, eh, what?" observed Allenby.

"To be sure," said Z. He tugged at Parr's sleeve. "Commissioner."

"What now?" demanded Parr, turning like a large elephant baited by a very small dog.

"Arrest that man," said Z, pointing to MacHussein.

"What for?" sputtered Parr.

"On suspicion."

"Suspicion of what? Who's suspicious of him?"

"I am," said Z with a sinister overtone.

"Now listen," screamed Parr, "that man was attacked himself—"

"Aha!" said Z. "That proves it."

"Proves what?"

"My suspicions."

"What suspicions?"

"None of your business," said Z, looking distrustfully at the Commissioner.

"My dear sir," broke in Idebar, "may I inquire what this is all about?"

Z turned to Allenby. "May he?"

"It should be referred to the home office," said Allenby. "But a field agent has to stick his neck out now and then, what? Damme, I *will* stick my neck out. He may."

"Go ahead, Your Excellency," bowed Z.

"I *was* going ahead," choked Idebar. "Mister . . . Mr. Jones, will you do something about these—these—"

"Allenby, what's the meaning of this?" gasped Alex.

The elegantly dressed Hoka extracted a handkerchief from his pocket and flicked invisible dust from his sleeve. "My dear old mangel-wurzel," he said, "must we do *all* the work? We have ransacked three suites, issued a mysterious warning, questioned eighteen members of the hostel staff, decoded thirty-four documents, and gathered everyone here for the dénouement. Having done this, we now sit back and wait for you to do what is yours to wit, reveal what is behind all this." He beamed, took a pinch of snuff, and added to MacHussein: "Sorry, old chap.You played the Great Game well."

The Bagdadburgian grinned and shrugged. "Let's get this over with, Commissioner," he suggested. "I could use some sleep."

Alex's brain leapfrogged. "Hey!" he cried.

"Arrest Jones," said Parr to the IBI agents. "I'll take the responsibility."

"Hold on there!" said Alex. He was still panting and shivering with the revelation that had burst on him. "Parr, I told you there was an illegal contract between Idebar and Tantho. That's the truth—and I now know where it is!"

"Oh, Alex," crooned Zuleika.

The man flung his arm dramatically out. The effect was somewhat spoiled by his knocking over a floor lamp, and in any event it is difficult to cut a heroic figure in a bathrobe, but he pointed at MacHussein and said with triumph: "You've got it!"

"You're raving!" said Idebar.

"Not very well trained in elocution, is he?" whispered Allenby to Marlowe.

"No," agreed the Hoka writer. "The proper phrase is, of course: 'You're mad, I tell you—mad, mad!' "

Alex backed away, speaking fast, as the IBI men closed in. "MacHussein isn't a human at all. He's a Worbenite. Do a little surgery on a Worbenite, he'll look just like an Arab. I can prove it. When he woke up, he used a Worbenite oath; I'd heard Idebar use it earlier. Well, anyone could do that, of course, but it's one point. Then Zulei—Her Excellency said he had been a perfect gentleman in all the years of working closely with her. And she was holding his head in a very, uh, comfortable position—but he sat up immediately and said he felt fine. Does that sound like a *human* male? Finally, when we broke in here just now it was quite dark, but he went right to the decanter and drank from it. How could he know it was brandy and not the jithna drink which would poison a human? The answer is, he couldn't . . . and he didn't care, because he's immune!"

"I really feel sorry for anyone in your mental state, Jones," purred Idebar. "Why, MacHussein himself was stunned."

"Yes." Alex was backed into a corner now. He picked up the lamp and used it to fend off the IBI agents. "That was to divert Zuleika's growing suspicion from him and make us look bad to Parr. You must have been alarmed when your suite was raided, and been fairly sure the Hokas did it, so you wanted us under suspicion and therefore, you hoped, immobilized. Actually, MacHussein was planted on Bagdadburgh years ago, to work his way up and be in a position to thwart—Leggo there!" He wrested the lamp from an agent's hand and swatted him.

"I shall file an official protest against your unbridled language," said Tantho with dignity.

Bert took out his giant burglar tool, joggled Prince Idebar's elbow, and tried to interest the elder statesman in a lecture on lockpicking.

"You knew Zuleika's agents would be trying to get that document," went on Alex. "You knew they might find it in any hiding place or waylay anyone carrying it—except one person, their own trusted comrade, Mac-Hussein! He's carrying it right now!"

The dark-faced man sneered and turned to go. "I won't bother answering that," he said. "Goodnight."

It was a mistake. Allenby made a beautiful flying tackle, shouting something about the playing fields of Eton. Bert picked him up by the ankles and shook him. And as he lay dazed, Z extracted the paper with a grand flourish and snapped it before Parr's eyes.

There was a long silence.

"Well?" said Parr when he had finished reading.

"Sleight-of-hand," blustered Tantho. "Planted on him."

Idebar nodded, elevating his brows. "There is also the matter of diplomatic immunity," he said in an ice-slick voice.

Parr reddened. "Yes," he said. "There is. I

can't do anything to punish you—nobody can. But I can tell the Council what I saw. That will settle who gets Goldfarb's Planet." He bowed heavily at Alex. "My apologies, Plenipotentiary Jones. I shall file an account of this daring exploit in your already distinguished record and, of course, recommend Toka for upgrading. Good evening, gentlebeings."

He went out. His IBI troop followed. There was another silence, broken only by Alex's wheezing. This was choked off by a long and passionate kiss, after which it resumed somewhat more noisily.

Prince Idebar stalked up to him. "Congratulations," he said with a vitriolic note. "You have, ah—"

"—foiled me," suggested Marlowe.

"Thank you. You have foiled—"

"Perhaps 'checkmated'?"

"Checkmated me, then. Thank you!" gritted Prince Idebar.

"Quite all right," said Marlowe.

"Jones," said Idebar, "you have won. But I am not without influence, even now, and I shall certainly not let you continue your career unmolested."

Alex smiled sweetly. "I have diplomatic immunity," he said.

"If you think that will help—"

"I think it will . . . Iddykins."

The Worbenite started. "What?"

"Iddykins," said Alex. "There is the little matter of your winter underwear, Iddykins.

Tell me, are you wearing it now? You have a very devoted wife, Iddykins, and I can think of several news services which would be happy to print a sample of her devotion . . . shall we say, a letter?"

"Um . . . yes." Idebar's aristocratic face purpled. "You do have the upper hand, it seems. Very well, sir." He stalked out, his tail lashing his ankles.

Tantho the Hairy started to follow. Alex grabbed his arm and pointed to the semiconscious MacHussein. "Better take him along," advised the human. "He's no more use to you, and might as well return to Worben. They can regenerate his normal appearance there."

Zuleika giggled. "I imagine," she said, "he'll be the first humanoid male in history who actually wanted to grow horns."

Alex blushed and led his Hokas out. Zuleika looked as if she might continue that line of thought, and he valued his own marriage.

Full Pack
(Hokas Wild)

When one is a regular ambassador to a civilized planet with full membership in the Interbeing League, it is quite sufficient to marry a girl who is only blond and beautiful. However, a plenipotentiary, guiding a backward world along the tortuous path to modern culture and full status, needs a wife who is also competent to handle the unexpected.

Alexander Jones had no reason to doubt that his Tanni met all the requirements of blondness, beauty, and competence. Neither did she. After a dozen years of Toka, he did not hesitate to leave her in charge while he took a native delegation to Earth and arranged for the planet's advancement in grade. And for a while things went smoothly—as smoothly, at least, as they can go on a world of eager, energetic teddy bears with imaginations active to the point of autohypnosis.

Picture her, then, on a sunny day shortly after lunch, walking through her official residence in the city Mixumaxu. Bright sunshine streamed through the glassite wall, revealing a pleasant view of cobbled streets, peaked roofs, and the grim towers of the Bastille. (This was annually erected by a self-appointed Roi Soleil, and torn down again by happy sans-culottes every July 14.) Tanni Jones' brief tunic and long golden hair were in the latest Bangkok fashion, even on this remote outpost, and her slim tanned figure would never be outmoded and she was comfortably aware of the fact. She had just checked the nursery, finding her two younger children safe at play. A newly arrived letter from her husband was tucked into her bosom. It announced in one sentence that his mission had been successful; thereafter several pages were devoted to more important matters, such as his imminent return with a new fur coat and he wished he could have been in the envelope and meanwhile he loved her madly, passionately, etc. She was murmuring to herself. Let us listen.

"Damn and blast it to hell, anyway! Where *is* that little monster?"

As she passed the utility room, a small, round-bellied, yellow-furred ursinoid popped out. This was Carruthers. His official title was Secretary-in-Chief-to-the-Plenipotentiary, which meant whatever Carruthers decided it should mean. Tanni felt relieved that today he was dressed merely in anachronistic trousers, spats, coat, and bowler hat, umbrella furled

beneath one arm, and spoke proper Oxford English. Last week it had been a toga, and he had brought her messages written in Latin with Greek characters; he had also button-holed every passerby with the information that she, Tanni, was above suspicion.

"The newsfax sheet, madam," he bowed. "Just came off the jolly old printer, don't y'know."

"Oh. Thanks." She took the bulletin and swept her eyes down it. Sensational tidings from Earth Headquarters: the delegates from Worben and Porkelans accused of conspiracy; Goldfarb's Planet awarded to Bagdadburgh; a League-wide alert for a Starflash space yacht which had been seen carrying the Tertiary Receptacle of Wisdom of Sanussi and the as-yet-unidentified dastards who had kidnaped him from his planet's Terrestrial embassy; commercial agreement governing the xisfthikl traffic signed between Jruthn and Ptrfsk— Tanni handed it back. There were too many worlds for anyone to remember; none of the names meant a thing to her.

"Have you seen young Alex?" she inquired.

Carruthers screwed a monocle into one beady black eye and tapped his short muzzle with the umbrella handle. "Why, yes, I do believe so, eh, what, what, what?"

"Well, where is he?"

"He asked me not to tell, madam." Carruthers eyed her reproachfully. "Couldn't peach on him, now could I? Old School Tie and all that sort of bally old . . ."

Tanni stalked off with the secretary still bleating behind her. True, she thought, her children did attend the same school which educated the adult Hokas, but . . . Hah! In a way, it was too bad Alex was returning so soon. She had long felt that he didn't take a firm enough line with his mercurial charges. He was too easily reduced to gibbering bewilderment. Now she was made of sterner stuff, and—in a Boadicean mood, she swept through a glassite passageway to the flitter garage.

Yes, there was her oldest son, Alexander Braithwaite Jones, Jr., curled up on the front seat with his nose buried in an ancient but well-preserved folio volume. She much regretted giving it to him. Her idea had been that he could carry it under one arm and enjoy it between bouts of healthful outdoor play, rather than having to sit hunched over a microset; but all he did was read it, sneaking off to places like—

"Alexander!"

The boy, a nine-year-old, tanglehaired pocket edition of his father, started guiltily. "Oh, hello, Mom," he smiled. It quite melted her resolve.

"Now, Alex," said Tanni in a reasonable tone, "you know you ought to be out getting some exercise. You've already read those *Jungle Books* a dozen times."

"Aw, golly, Mom," protested the younger generation. "You give me a book and then you won't let me read it!"

"*Alexander!*" Boadicea had returned in full

119

armor. "You know perfectly well what I mean. Now I told you to—"

"Madam," squeaked a voice, "the devil's to pay!"

Tanni yipped and jumped. Remembering herself, she turned in a suitably dignified manner to see Carruthers, hastily clad in pith helmet and fake walrus mustache.

"Message on the transtype just came," said the Hoka. "From Injah, don't y' know. Seems a bit urgent."

Tanni snatched the paper he extended and read:

> FROM: *Captain O'Neil of the Black Tyrone*
> TO: *Rt. Hon. Plen. A. Jones*
> SUBJECT: *UFO (Unidentified Flying Object) identified. Your Excellency:*
>
> *While burying dead and bolting beef north of the Kathun road, received word from native scout of UFO crashed in jungle nearby, containing three beasts of unknown origin. Interesting, what?*
> *Yr. Humble & Obt. Svt., etc.,*
> *"Crook" O'Neil*

For a moment Tanni had a dreamlike sense of unreality. Then, slowly, she translated the Hokaese. Yes . . . there were some Hokas from this northern hemisphere who had moved down to the sub-continent due south which the native had gleefully rechristened India, and set themselves up as Imperialists. The

120

Indians were quite happy to cooperate, since
it meant that they could wear turbans and
mysterious expressions. Vaguely she recalled
Kipling's _Ballad of Boh Da Thone._ It dealt
with Burma, to be sure, but if consistency is
the virtue of little minds, then the Hokas were
very large-minded indeed. India was mostly
Kipling country, with portions here and there
belonging to Clive, the Grand Mogul, and lesser
lights.

The UFO must be a spaceship and the
"beasts," of course, its crew, from some other
planet. God alone knew what they would think
if the Indians located them first and assumed
they were—_what_ would Hokas convinced they
were Hindus, Pathans, and Britishers imagine alien space travelers to be?

"Carruthers!" said Tanni sharply. "Has there
been any distress call on the radio?"

"No, madam, there has not. And damme, I
don't like it. Don't like it at all. When I was
with Her Majesty's Very Own Royal, Loyal,
and Excessively Brave Fifth Fusiliers, I—"

Tanni's mind worked swiftly. This was just
the sort of situation in which Alex, Sr., was
always getting involved and coming off second best. It was her chance to show him how
these matters ought to be handled.

"Carruthers," she snapped, "you and I will
take the flitter and go to the rescue of these
aliens. And I want it clearly understood that—"

"_Mom!_ Can I go? Can I go, huh, Mom, can
I?"

122

It was Alex, Jr., hopping up and down with excitement, his eyes shining.

"No," began Tanni. "You stay here and read your book and—" She checked herself, aware of the pitfall. Countermanding her own orders! Here was a heaven-sent opportunity to get the boy out of the house and interested in something new—like, for example, these castaways. They were clearly beings of authority or means, important beings, or they could not afford a private spaceship. There was no danger involved; Toka's India was a land of congenial climate, without any life-forms harmful to man.

"You can go," she told Alex severely, "if you'll do exactly as I say at all times. Now that means exactly.' "

"Yes, yes, yes. Sure, Mom, sure."

"All right, then," said Tanni. She ran back into the house, making hasty arrangements with the servants, while Carruthers set the flitter's autopilot to locating the British bivouac. In minutes two humans and one Hoka were skyborne.

The camp proved to be a collection of tents set among fronded trees and tangled vines, drowsy under the late afternoon sun. A radio and a transtype were the only modern equipment, a reluctant concession to the plenipotentiary's program of technological education. They stood at the edge of the clearing, covered with jungle mold, while the Black Tyrone,

123

a hundred strong, drilled with musket, fife, and drum.

Captain O'Neil was a grizzled, hard-bitten Hoka in shorts, tunic, and bandolier. He limped across the clearing, pith helmet in hand, as Tanni emerged from the flitter with Alex and Carruthers.

"Honored, ma'am," he bowed. "Pardon my one-sided gait, ma'am. Caught a slug in the ulnar bone recently." (Tanni knew very well he had not; there was no war on Toka, and anyway the ulnar bone is in the arm.) "Now a slug that is hammered from telegraph wire— ah, a book?"

His eyes lit up with characteristic enthusiasm, and Tanni, looking around, discovered the reason in her son's arms.

"Alex!" she said. "Did you bring that *Jungle Books* thing along?" His downcast face told her that he had. "I'm not going to bother with it any longer. You hand that right over to Captain O'Neil and let him keep it for you till we leave for home again."

"Awwwww, Mom!"

"Right now!"

"—is a thorn in the flesh and a rankling fire," murmured Captain O'Neil. "Ah, thank you, m'boy. Well, well, what have we here? *The Jungle Books,* by Rudyard Kipling himself! Never seen 'em before." Humming a little tune, he opened the volume.

"Now, where is that UFO?" demanded Tanni. "Have you rescued its crew yet?"

"No, ma'am," said the Captain, with his

nose between the pages. "Going to go look for 'em this morning, but we were hanging Danny Deever and—" His voice trailed off into a mumble.

Tanni compressed her lips. "Well, we shall have to find them," she clipped. "Is it far? Should we go overland or take the flitter?"

"Er . . . yes, ma'am? Ha, hum," said O'Neil, closing the book reluctantly but marking the place with a furry forefinger. "Not far. Overland, I would recommend. You'd find landing difficult in our jungles here in the Seeonee Hills—"

"The what?"

"Er . . . I mean north of the Kathun road. A wolf . . . I mean, a native scout brought us the word. Perhaps you'd care to talk to him, ma'am?"

"I would," said Tanni. "Right away."

O'Neil shouted for Gunga Din and sent him off to look, then dove back into the volume. Presently another Hoka slouched from behind a tent. He was of the local race, which had fur of midnight black, but was otherwise indistinguishable from the portly northern variety. Unless, of course, you specified his costume: turban, baggy trousers, loose shirt, assorted cutlery thrust into a sash, and a flaming red false beard. He salaamed.

"What's your name?" asked Tanni.

"Mahbub Ali, memsahib," replied the newcomer. "Horse trader."

"You saw the ship land?"

"Yes, memsahib. I had stopped to patch my bridles and count my gear—whee, a book!"

"It's mine!" said O'Neil, pulling it away from him.

"Oh. Well, ah—" Mahbub Ali edged around so that he could read over the Captain's shoulder. "I, er, saw the thing flash through the air and went to see. I, um, glimpsed three beasts of a new sort coming out, but, um, they were back inside before I could . . . By that time the moon was shining into the cave where I lived and I said to myself, 'Augrh!' I said, 'it is time to hunt again—' "

"Gentlebeings!" cried Tanni. The book snapped shut and two fuzzy faces looked dreamily up at her. "I shall want the regiment to escort me to that ship tomorrow."

"Why, er, to be sure, ma'am," said O'Neil vaguely. "I'll tell the pack and we'll move out at dawn."

A couple of extra tents were set up in the clearing, and there was a supper at which the humans shared top honors with Danny Deever. (A Hoka's muscles are so strong that hanging does not injure him.) When night fell, with subtropical swiftness, Alex crawled into one tent and Tanni into the other. She lay for a while, thinking cheerfully that her theories of management were bearing fruit. True, there had been some small waverings on the part of the autochthones, but she had kept things rolling firmly in the proper direction. Why in the Galaxy did her husband insist it was so difficult to . . .

The last thing she remembered as she drifted into sleep was the murmur of a voice from the campfire. "Crook" O'Neil had assembled his command and was reading to them. . . .

She blinked her eyes open to dazzling sunlight. Dawn was hours past, and a great stillness brooded over the clearing. More indignant than alarmed, she scrambled out of her sleeping bag, threw on tunic and shoes, and went into the open.

The camp was deserted. Uniforms and equipment were piled by the cold ashes of the fire, and a flying snake was opening a can of bully beef with its saw-edged beak. For a moment the world wavered before her.

"Alex!" she screamed.

Running from tent to tent, she found them all empty. She remembered wildly that she did not even have a raythrower along. Sobbing, she dashed toward the flitter—get an aerial view—

Bush crackled, and a round black-nosed head thrust cautiously forth. Tanni whirled, blinked, and recognized the gray-shot pelt of O'Neil.

"Captain!" she gasped. "What's happened? Come out this minute!"

The brush parted, and the Hoka trotted out on all fours, attired in nothing but his own fur.

"Captain O'Neil!" wailed Tanni. "What's the meaning of this?"

The native reached up, got the hem of her tunic between his jaws, and tugged. Then he

let go and moved toward the canebrake, looking back at her.

"Captain," said Tanni helplessly. She followed him for a moment, but stopped. Her voice grew shrill. "I'm not moving another centimeter till you explain this—this outrageous—" The Hoka waddled back to her. "Well, speak up! Don't whine at me! Stand up and talk like a . . . like a . . . a Captain. *And stop licking my hand!*"

O'Neil headed into the jungle. Tanni gave up. Throttling her fears, she went after him. Colorful birds whistled overhead, and flowers drooped on long vines and snagged in her hair. Presently she found herself on a trail. It ran for some two kilometers, an uneventful trip except for the pounding of her heart and the Captain's tendency to dash off after small game.

At the end, they reached a meadow surrounding a large flat-topped rock. The Black Tyrone were there. Like their commander, they had stripped off their uniforms and now frisked about in the grass, tumbling like puppies and snarling between their teeth. She caught fragments of continuous conversation:

"—Sambhur belled, once, twice, and again . . . wash daily from nose-tip to tail-tip . . . the meat is very near the bone—" and other interesting though possibly irrelevant information.

Rolling about, Tanni's eyes found her son. He was seated on top of the rock, wearing only a wreath of flowers and a kitchen knife on a string about his neck. At his feet, equally nude and happy, sprawled Carruthers and the black-furred Mahbub Ali.

"Alex!" cried Tanni. She sped to the rock and stared up at her offspring, uncertain whether to kiss and cry over him or turn him across her knee. "What are you doing here?"

Captain O'Neil spoke for the first time. "Thy mother was doubtful about coming, Little Frog."

"Oh, so you *can* talk!" said Tanni, glaring at him.

"He can't talk to you, Mom," said Alex.

"What do you mean, he can't?"

"But that's wolf talk, Mom. You can't understand it. I'll have to translate for you."

"Wolf?"

"The Seeonee Pack," said Alex proudly. He nodded at O'Neil. "Thou hast done well, Akela."

"Argh!" said Mahbub Ali. "*I* run with no pack, Little Frog."

"By the Bull that brought me!" exclaimed Alex, contrite. "I forgot, Bagheera." He stroked the black head. "This is Bagheera, Mom, the Black Panther, you know." Pointing to the erstwhile Carruthers: "And this is Baloo the Bear. And I'm Mowgli. Isn't it terrific, Mom?"

"No, it isn't!" snapped Tanni. Now, if ever, was the time to take the strong line she believed in. "Captain O'Neil, will you stop being Akela this minute? I'm here to rescue some very important people, and—"

"What says thy mother Messua?" asked the

Captain—or, rather, Akela—lolling out his tongue and looking at Mowgli-Alex.

The boy started gravely to translate.

"Alex, stop that!" Tanni found her voice wobbling. "Don't encourage him in this . . . this game!"

"But it isn't a game, Mom," protested her son. "It's real. Honest!"

"You know it isn't," scolded Tanni. "He's not really Akela at all. He should be sensible and go back to being himself."

"Himself?" murmured Baloo-Carruthers, forgetting in his surprise that he wasn't supposed to understand English.

"Captain O'Neil," explained Tanni, holding on to her patience with both hands. "Captain—"

"But he wasn't really Captain O'Neil either," pointed out Baloo.

On many occasions Tanni had listened sympathetically, but with a hidden sense of superiority, to her husband's description of his latest encounter with Hoka logic. She had never really believed in all the dizzy sensations he spoke of. Now she felt them. She gasped feebly and sat down in the grass.

"I wanted to let you know, Mom," chattered Alex. "The Pack's got Shere Khan treed a little ways from here. I wanted to know if it was all right for me to go call him a Lame Thief of the Waingunga. Can I, Mom, huh, can I?"

Tanni drew a long, shuddering breath. She remembered Alex, Sr.'s advice: 'Roll with the punches. Play along and watch for a chance

to use their own logic on them." There didn't seem to be anything else to do at the moment. "All right," she whispered.

Akela took the lead, yapping; Baloo and Bagheera closed in on either side of Alex; and the Pack followed. Brush crackled. It was not easy for a naturally bipedal species to go on all fours, and Tanni saw Akela walking erect when he thought she wasn't looking. He caught her eye, blushed under his fur, and crouched down again.

She decided that this new lunacy would prove rather unstable. It just wasn't practical to run around on your hands and try to bring down game with your teeth. But it would probably take days for the Hokas to weary of the sport and return to being the Black Tyrone, and meanwhile what was she to do?

"By the Broken Lock that freed me!" exclaimed Bagheera, coming to a halt. "One approaches—I mean approacheth."

"Two approach," corrected Baloo, sitting up on his haunches bear-fashion. Being an ursinoid, he did this rather well.

Tanni looked ahead. Through a clump of bamboo-like plants emerged a black-haired form with a blunt snout under heavy brow ridges, the size of a man but stooped over, long arms dangling past bent knees. He wore a sadly stained and ragged suit. She recognized him as a native of the full-status planet Chakba. Behind him lifted the serpentine head of a being from some world unknown to her.

Akela bristled. "The Bandar-log!" he snarled.

"But see," pointed Baloo, "Kaa the Python follows him, and yet the shameless Bandar is not afraid." He scratched his head. "This is not supposed to be," he said plaintively.

The Chakban spotted Tanni and hurried toward her. "Ah, dear lady," he cried. His voice was highpitched, but he spoke fluent English. "At last, a civilized face!" He bowed. "Permit me to introduce myself. I am Echpo of Doralik-Li, and my poor friend is named Seesis."

Tanni, glancing at the friend in question, was moved to agree that he was, indeed, poor. Seesis had come into full view now, revealing ten meters of snake body, limbless except for two delicate arms just under the big bald head. A pair of gold-rimmed pince-nez wobbled on his nose. He hissed dolefully and undulated toward the woman, wringing his small hands.

Tanni gave her name and asked: "Are you the beings who crashlanded here?"

"Yes, dear lady," said Echpo. "A most—"

Seesis tugged at the woman's tunic and began to scratch on the ground with his forefinger.

"What?" Tanni bent over to look.

"Poor chap, poor chap," said Echpo, shaking his head. "He doesn't speak English, you know. Moreover, the crash . . ." He revolved a finger near his own right temple and gave her a meaningful look.

"Oh, how terrible!" Tanni got to her feet in spite of Seesis' desperate efforts to hold her down and make her look at his dirt scratchings. "We'll have to get him to a doctor—Dr.

Arrowsmith in Mixumaxu is really very good if I can drag him away from discovering bacteriophage—"

"That is not necessary, madam," said Echpo. "Seesis will recover naturally. I know his race. But if I may presume upon your kindness, we do need transportation."

The Hokas crowded around Seesis, addressing him as Kaa and asking him if he was casting his skin and obliterating his marks on the ground. The herpetoid seemed ready to burst into tears.

"But weren't there three of you?" asked Tanni.

"Yes, indeed," said Echpo. "But—well—I am afraid, dear lady, that your little friends do not seem to approve of our companion Heragli. They have, er, chased him up a tree."

"Why, how could they?" Gently, Tanni detached the fingers of Seesis from her skirt, patted him on his scaly head, and turned an accusing eye on Alex. "Young man, what do you know about this?"

The boy squirmed. "That must be Shere Khan." Defiantly: "He does look like a tiger too." He glared at Echpo. "Believe thou not the Bandar-log."

"These gentlebeings are no such thing!" snapped Tanni.

"Surely thy mother has been bitten by Tabaqui, the Jackal," said Baloo to Alex. "All the Jungle knows Shere Khan."

"This is *dewanee*, the madness," agreed

Bagheera. "Heed thy old tutor who taught thee the Law, Little Frog."

"But—" began Alex. "But the hairy one dares say that—"

"Surely, Little Brother," interrupted Baloo, "thou hast learned by this time to take no notice of the Bandar-log. They have no Law. They are very many, evil, dirty, shameless, and they desire, if they have any fixed desire, to be noticed by the Jungle-People. But we do *not* notice them even when they throw nuts and filth on our heads."

"Oh!" groaned Echpo. "That I, an ex-cabinet minister of the Chakban Federation, B.A., M.S., Ph.D., LL.D., graduate of Hasolbath, Trmp, and the Sorbonne, should be accused of throwing nuts and filth on people's heads to attract attention!"

"I'm *so* sorry!" apologized Tanni. "It's the imagination these Hokas have. Please, please forgive them, sir!"

"Your slightest whim, dear lady, is my most solemn command and highest joy," bowed Echpo.

Tanni returned gallantly to the subject: "But how did you happen to be marooned here?"

"Ah . . . we were outward bound, madam, on a mission from Earth to the Rim Stars." Echpo produced a box of lozenges and politely offered them around. "A cultural mission, headed by our poor friend Seesis—is he bothering you, dear lady? Just slap his hands down. The shock, you know . . . Ah . . . A most important and urgent mission, I may say with all due modesty, undertaken to—pardon me, I cannot say more. Our converter began giving trouble as we passed near this sun, so we approached your planet—Toka, is that the name?—to get help. We knew from the pilot's manual that it had civilization, though we scarcely expected such delightful company as yours. At any rate, the converter failed us completely as we were entering the atmosphere, and though we glided down, the landing was still hard enough to wreck our communications equipment. That was yesterday, and today we were setting out in quest of help—we had seen from the air that there is a city some fifty kilometers hence—when, ah, your Hokas appeared and our poor friend Heragli—"

"Oh, dear!" said Tanni. "We'd better go get him right away. Can you guide me?"

"I should be honored," said Echpo. "I know the very tree."

"Does thy mother hunt with the Bandarlog, O Mowgli?" inquired Akela.

"Certainly not!" snapped Tanni, whirling on him. "You ought to be ashamed of yourself, Captain."

"What says she?" asked Akela agreeably.

Alex repeated it for him.

"Oh!" said Tanni, stamping off.

'Ah . . . poor dear Seesis," murmured Echpo. "He should not be left unguarded. He could hurt himself. Would your, ah, Hokas watch him while we rescue Heragli?"

"Of course," said Tanni. "Alex, you stay here and see to it."

139

The boy protested, was *Alexander*'d down, and gave in and announced importantly that he, the Man-Cub, wished the Pack to remain with him and not let Kaa depart. Tanni and Echpo started into the woods. Baloo and Bagheera followed.

"Hey, there!" said the woman. "Didn't Mowgli tell you to—"

"By the Broken Lock that freed me," squeaked Bagheera, slapping his paunch with indignation, "dost thou take *us* for wolves?"

Tanni sighed and traded a glance with Echpo. As they went among the trees, she calmed down enough to say: "I can fly you to Mixumaxu, of course, and put you up; but it may take weeks before you can get off the planet. Not many deep-space ships stop here."

"Oh, dear." The Chakban wrung hairy hands. "Our mission is *so* vital. Could we not even get transportation to Gelkar?"

"Well . . ." Tanni considered. "Why, yes, it's only a few lightyears off. I can take you myself in our courier boat, and you can charter a ship there."

"Blessed damosel, my gratitude knows no limits," said Echpo.

Tanni preened herself. She was no snob, but certainly a favor done for beings as important as these would hurt no one's career.

Through the ruffling leaves, she heard a hoarse, angry bellow. "That must be your friend," she remarked brightly, or as brightly as possible when battling through a humid

140

jungle with hair uncombed and no breakfast. "What did you say his name was?"

"Heragli. A Rowra of Drus. A most gentlemanly felino-centauroid, dear lady. I can't conceive why your Hokas insist on chasing him up trees."

A minute later the girl saw him, perched in the branches seven meters above ground. She had to admit that he was not unlike a tiger. The long, black-striped orange body was there, and the short yellow-eyed head, though a stumpy torso with two muscular arms was between. His whiskers were magnificent, and a couple of saber teeth did the resemblance no harm. Like Echpo, he wore the thorn-ripped tatters of a civilized business suit.

"Heragli, dear friend," called the Chakban, "I have found a most agreeable lady who has graciously promised to help us."

"Are those unprintables around?" floated down a bass rumble. "Every blanked time I set foot to earth, the thus-and-so's have gone for me."

"It's all right!" snapped Tanni. She was not, she told herself, a prude; but Heragli's language was scarcely what she had been led to expect from the Bandar's—oops!—from Echpo's description of him as a most gentlemanly felino-centauroid.

"Why, sputter dash censored!" rasped the alien. "I see two of 'em just behind you!"

"Oh, them?" said Tanni. "Never mind them. They're only a bear and a black panther."

"They're *what*?"

"They're . . . well . . . oh, never mind! Come on down."

Heragli descended, two meters of rippling muscle hot in the leaf-filtered sunlight. "Very well, very well," he grumbled. "But I don't trust 'em. Lick my weight in flaming wildcats, but these asterisk unmentionables wreck my nerves. Where's the snake?"

Echpo winced. "My dear fellow!" he protested delicately.

"All right, all right!" bawled the Rowra. "The herpetoid, then. Don't hold with these dashed euphemisms. Call an encarnadined spade a cursed spade is my way. Where is he?"

"We left him back at—"

"Should've knocked'm on the mucking head. Said so all along. Save all this deleted trouble."

Echpo flinched again. "The, ah, the Rowra is an old military felino-centauroid," he explained hastily. "Believes in curing shock with counter-shock. Isn't that right, Heragli?"

"What? What're you babbling about now? Oh . . . oh, yes. Your servant, ma'am," thundered the other. "Which bleeding way out, eh?"

"A rough exterior, dear lady," whispered Echpo in Tanni's ear, "but a heart of gold."

"That may be," answered the woman sharply, "but I'm going to have to ask him to moderate his voice and expurgate his language. What if the Hokas should hear him?"

"Blunderbore and killecrantz!" swore Heragli. "Let'm hear. I've had enough of this deifically anathematized tree climbing. Let'm show up once more and I'll gut 'em, I'll skin 'em, I'll—"

A chorus of falsetto wolfish howls interrupted him, and a second later the space around the tree was filled with leaping, yelling Hokas and the Rowra was up in the branches again.

"Come down, Striped Killer!" bawled Akela, bounding a good two meters up the trunk. "Come down ere I forget wolves cannot climb! I myself will tear thy heart out!"

"Sput! Meowr!" snarled Heragli, swiping a taloned paw at him. "Meeourl spss rowul rhnrrrr!"

"What's he saying?" demanded Tanni.

"Dear lady," replied Echpo with a shudder, "don't ask. General! General!—His old rank may snap him out of it—General, remember your duty!"

"LAME THIEF OF THE WAINGUNGA!" shouted Alex, bombarding him with fallen fruits.

Heragli closed his eyes and panted. "Oh, m'nerves!" he gasped above the roar of the Hokas. "All your fault, Echpo, you insisting on no sidearms. Of all the la-di-da conspir—"

"*General!*" cried the Chakban.

Tanni struggled around the Hokas and collared her son. "Alex," she said ominously, "I told you to keep them away."

"But they outvoted me, Mom," he answered. "They're the Free People, you know, and it's the full Pack—"

"FOR THE PACK, FOR THE FULL PACK,

IT IS MET!'' chorused the Hokas, leaping up and snapping at Heragli's tail.

Tanni put her hands over her ears and tried to think. It hurt her pride, but she sought desperately to imagine what Alex, Sr., would have done. Play along with them . . . use their own fantasy . . . yes and she had read the *Jungle Books* herself—Ah!

She snatched a nut from her boy just before he launched it and said sweetly: "Alex, dear, shouldn't the Pack be in bed now?"

"Huh, Mom?"

"Doesn't the Law of the Jungle say so? Ask Baloo."

"Indeed, Man-Cub," replied Baloo pontifically when Alex had repeated it, "the Law of the Jungle specifically states: 'And remember the night is for hunting, and forget not the day is for sleep.' Now that you remind me—thou remindest me, it is broad daylight and all the wolves ought to be in their lairs."

It took a little while to calm down the Hokas, but then they trotted obediently off into the forest. Tanni was a bit disconcerted to note that Baloo and Bagheera were still present. She racked her brains for something in the *Jungle Books* specifically dealing with the obligation of bears and black panthers also to go off and sleep in the daytime. Nothing, however, came to mind. And Heragli refused to climb down while—

Inspiration came. She turned to the last Hokas. "Aren't you thirsty?" she asked.

"What says thy mother, Little Frog?" demanded Bagheera, washing his nose with his hand and trying to purr.

"She asked if thou and Baloo were not thirsty," said Alex.

"Thirsty?" The two Hokas looked at each other. The extreme suggestibility of their race came into play. Two tongues reached out and licked two muzzles.

"Indeed, the Rains have been scant this year," agreed Bagheera.

"Perhaps I had better go shake the *mohwa* tree and check the petals that fall down," said Baloo.

"I hear," said the girl slyly, "that Hathi proclaimed the Water Truce last night."

"Oh . . . *ah?*" said Bagheera.

"And you know that according to the Law of the Jungle, that means all the animals must drink peaceably together," went on Tanni. "Tell them, Alex."

"Quite true," nodded Baloo sagely when the boy had translated. "Macmillan edition, 1933, page 68."

"So," said Tanni, springing her trap, "you'll have to take Shere Khan off and let him drink with you."

"*Wuh!*" said Baloo, sitting down on his haunches to consider the situation. "It is the Law," he decided at length.

"You can come down now," called Tanni to Heragli. "They won't hurt you."

"Blood and bones!" grumbled the Rowra, but descended and looked at the Hokas with a noticeable lack of enthusiasm. "Har d'ja do."

"Hello, Lame Thief," said Bagheera amiably.

"*Lame Thief?* Why—" Heragli began to roar, and Bagheera tried manfully to arch his back, which is not easy for a barrel-shaped Hoka.

"General! General!" interrupted Echpo. "It's the only way. Go off and have a drink with them, and as soon as you can, meet us here again."

"Oh, very well. Blank dash flaming etcetera." Heragli trotted off into the brush, accompanied by his foes. Their voices trailed back:

"Hast hunted recently, Striped Killer?"

"Eh? What? Hunted? Well, as a matter of fact, in England on Earth last month—the Quorn—Master of the Hunt told me—went to earth at—"

The jungle swallowed them up.

"And now, dear lady," said Echpo nervously, "I must presume still further upon your patience. Poor Seesis has been left unguarded all this time—"

"Oh, yes!" The woman's long slim legs broke into a trot, back toward the place where she had first met the herpetoid. Echpo lumbered beside her and Alex followed.

"Ah . . . it is a difficult situation," declared the Chakban. "I fear the concussion has made my valued friend Seesis, ah, distrust the General and myself. His closest comrades! Can you imagine? He has, I think, some strange delusion that we mean to harm him."

Tanni slowed down. She felt no great eagerness to confront a paranoid python.

"He won't get violent," reassured Echpo. "I just wanted to warn you to discount anything he may do. He might, for example, try to write messages . . . Ah, here we are!"

They looked around the trampled vegetation. "He must have slipped away," said Tanni. "But he can't have gone far."

"Oh, he can move rapidly when he chooses, gracious madam," said Echpo, rubbing his hands in an agitated fashion. "Normally, of course, he does not so choose. You see, his race places an almost fanatical emphasis on self-restraint. Dignity, honor, and the like . . . those are the important things. A code, dear lady, which"—Echpo's deep-set eyes took on an odd gleam—"renders them vulnerable to, er, manipulation by those alert enough to press the proper semantic keys. But one which also renders them quite unpredictable. We had better find him at once."

It was not a large area in which they stood, and it soon became apparent that they had not simply overlooked the presence of ten meters of snake-like alien. A shout from Alex brought them to a trail crushed into the soft green herbage, as if someone had dragged a barrel through it. "This," said the boy, "must be the road of Kaa."

"Excellent spotting, young man," said Echpo. "Let us follow it."

They went rapidly along the track for several minutes. Tanni brushed the tangled golden hair from her eyes and wished for a comb, breakfast, a hot bath and—She noticed that the trail suddenly bent northward and continued in a straight line, as if Kaa—Seesis, blast it!—had realized where he was and set off toward some definite goal.

Echpo stopped, frowning, his flat nostrils a-twitch. "Dear me," he murmured, "this is *most* distressing."

"Why—he's headed toward your ship, hasn't he?" asked Tanni. "He should be easy to find. Let's go!"

"Oh, no, no, no!" The Chakban shook his bat-eared head. "I wouldn't dream of letting you and your son—delightful boy, madam!—go any further. It is much too dangerous."

"Nonsense! There's nothing harmful here, and you said yourself he isn't violent."

"Please! Not another word!" The long hands waved her back. "No, dear lady, just return to the meeting place, if you will, and when Heragli gets there send him on to the ship. Meanwhile I will follow poor Seesis and, ah, do what I can."

Before Tanni could reply, Echpo had bounded off and the tall grasses hid him.

She stood for a moment, frowning. The Chakban was a curious and contradictory personality. Though his manners were impeccable, she had not felt herself warming to him. There was something, something almost . . . well, *Bandar-loggish* about him. *Ridiculous!* she told herself. *But why did he suddenly change*

*his mind about having me along? Just because
Seesis headed back toward the wrecked ship?*

"Shucks, Mom," pouted Alex, "everybody's
gone. All the wolves are in bed—in their lairs,
I mean, and Bagheera and Baloo gone off
with Shere Khan, and the Bandar's gone to
the Cold Lairs and we can't even watch Kaa
fight him. Nobody lets me have any fun."

Decision came to Tanni. The demented
Seesis might, after all, turn on Echpo. If she had
any chance of preventing such a catastrophe,
her duty was clear. In plain language, she felt
an infernal curiosity. "Come along, Alex," she
said.

They had not far to go. Breaking through a
tall screen of pseudo-bamboo, they looked out
on a meadow.

And in the center of that meadow rested a
small, luxurious Starflash space rambler.

"Wait here, Alex," ordered Tanni. "If there
seems to be any danger, run for help."

She crossed the ground to the open airlock.
Strange, the ship was not even dented. Peering in, she saw the control room. No sign of
Echpo or Seesis—maybe they were somewhere
aft. She entered.

It struck her that the controls were in very
good shape for a vessel that had landed hard
enough to knock out its communication gear.
On impulse, she went over to the visio and
punched its buttons. The screen lit up . . .
why, it was perfectly useable! She would call
Mixumaxu and have a detachment of Hoka

police flown here. The Private Eyes and Honest Cops could easily—

A thick, hairy arm shot past her and a long finger snapped the set off. Another arm like a great furry shackle pinned her into the chair she had taken.

"That," whispered Echpo, "was a mistake, dear lady."

For a second, instinctively and furiously, Tanni tried to break loose. A kitten might as well have tried to escape a gorilla. Echpo let her have it out while he closed the airlock by remote control. Then he eased his grip. She bounced from the chair. A hard hand grabbed her wrist and whirled her about.

"What is this?" she raged. "Let me *go!*" She kicked at Echpo's ankles. He slapped her so her head rang. Sobbing, she relaxed enough to stare at him through a blur of horror.

"I am afraid, dear Mrs. Jones, that you have penetrated our little deception," said the Chakban gently. "I had hoped we could abandon our ship here, since a description of it has unfortunately been broadcast on the subvisio. By posing as castaways, we could have used the transportation to Gelkar which you so graciously offered us, and hired another vessel there. But as it is—" He shrugged. "It seems best we stay with this one after all, using you, madam, as a hostage ... much though it pains me, of course."

"You wouldn't dare!" gasped Tanni, unable to think of a more telling remark.

"Dare? Dear lady," said Echpo, smiling, "our

poor friend Seesis is the Tertiary Receptacle of Wisdom of Sanussi. If we dared kidnap him, surely—Please hold still. It would deeply grieve me to have to bind you."

"Sanussi . . . I don't believe you," breathed the girl. "Why, you're unarmed and he must have twice your strength."

"Dear charmer," sighed Echpo, "how little you know of Sanussians. Their ethical code is *so* unreasonably strict. When Heragli and I entered Seesis' embassy office on Earth, all we had to do was threaten to fill an ancestral seltzer bottle we had previously . . . ah . . . borrowed, with soda pop. The dishonor would have compelled the next hundred generations of his family to spend an hour a day in ceremonial writhing and give up all public positions. We wrung his parole from him: he was not to speak to anyone or resist us with force until released."

"Not *speak* . . . oh, so that's why he was trying to write," said Tanni. A degree of steadiness was returning to her. She could not really believe this mincing dandy capable of harm. "And I suppose he slipped back here with some idea of calling our officials and showing them a written account of—"

"How quickly you grasp the facts, madam," bowed Echpo. "Naturally, I trailed him and, since he may not use his strength on me, dragged him into a stateroom aft and coiled him up. As long as Heragli and I abide by the Sanussian code—chiefly, to refrain from endangering others—he is bound by his promise.

153

That is why we have no weapons; the General
is so impulsive."

"But why have you kidnapped him?"

"Politics. A matter of pressure to get certain concessions from his planet. Don't trouble your pretty head about it, my lady. As
soon as practical after we have reached our
destination—surely not more than a year—you
will be released with our heartfelt thanks for
your invaluable assistance."

"But you don't need *me* for a hostage!"
wailed Tanni. "You've got Seesis himself."

"Tut-tut. The Sanussian police are hot on
our trail. Despite the size of interstellar space,
they may quite possibly detect us and close in
. . . after which, to wipe out the stain on *their*
honor, they would cheerfully blow Seesis up
with Heragli and myself. But their ethics will
not permit them to harm an innocent by-
stander like you, so—" Echpo backed toward
the airlock, half dragging the woman. His bulk
filled the chamber, blocking off escape, as he
opened the valves. "So, as soon as Heragli
returns—and not finding me at the agreed
rendezvous, he will surely come here—we
depart."

His simian face broke into a grin as discor-
dant noises floated nearer. "Why, here he is
now. Heragli, dear friend, do hurry. We must
leave this delightful planet immediately."

His voice carried to the Rowra, who had
just emerged from the canebrake with Bagheera
on one side and Baloo on the other. Staggering,
Heragli sat down, licked one oversized paw,

and began to wash his face. Peering past Echpo, Tanni saw that the General's swiping motions were rather unsteady.

"Heragli!" said the Chakban on a sharper note. "Pay attention!"

"Go sputz yourself," boomed the Rowra, and broke into song. "Oh, when I was twenty-one, when I was twenty-one, I never had lots of mvrouwing but I always had lots of fun. My basket days were over and my prowling days begun, on the very very rrnowing night when I was twenty-one—*Chorus!*" he roared, beating time with a wavering paw, and the two Hokas embraced him and chimed in: *"When we wash twenty-one—"*

"Heragli!" yelled Echpo. "What's wrong with you?"

Tanni could have told him. She realized suddenly, as she stood there with the Chakban's heavy grip on her wrist, that when she evoked thirst in Baloo and Bagheera, she had pointed them in one inevitable direction: the abandoned camp of the Black Tyrone. The phrase "take Shere Khan off and let him drink with you" could have only one meaning to a Hoka. Heragli, like many beings before him, had encountered the fiery Tokan liquor.

There are bigger, stronger, wiser races than the Hokas, but the Galaxy knows none with more capacity. Heragli was twice the size and eight times the weight of a Hoka, but his companions were just pleasantly high, while he was—no other word will do—potted. And

Tanni was willing to bet that Baloo and Bagheera were each two bottles ahead of him.

The General rolled over on his back and waved his feet in the air. "Oh, that little ball of yarn—" he warbled.

"Heragli!" shrieked Echpo.

"Oh, those wild, wild kittens, those wild, wild kittens, they're making a wildcat of me!"

"General!"

"Old tomcats never die, they just fa-a-a-ade—huh? Whuzza matta wi' you, monkey?" demanded Heragli, still on his back, looking at the spaceship upside down from bloodshot eyes. "Stannin' onna head. Riddickerluss, ab-so-lute-ly . . . Oh, curse the city that stole muh Kitty, by dawn she'll—Le's havva nuther one, mnowrr, 'fore you leave me! Hell an' damnation," said Heragli, suddenly dropping from the peak of joyous camaraderie to the valley of bitter suspicion, "dirty work inna catagon. Passed over f' promotion, twishe. Classmate, too . . . Is this a ray gun that I see b'fore me, the handle toward muh hand? Come, lemme clutch thee. . . . Monkeys an' snakes. Gallopin' horrors, I call 'em. Never trus' a primate—" and he faded off into mutterings.

"General!" called Echpo, sternly. "Pull yourself together and come aboard. We're leaving."

"Huh? Awri', awri', awri'—" said Heragli in a bleared tone. He lurched to all four feet, focused with some effort on the ship, and wobbled in its general direction.

"Mom!" cried a boyish voice, and Alex broke into the meadow. "What's going on?" He spotted Tanni with Echpo's hand clutching her. "What're you doing to my mother?"

"Heragli!" yelped Echpo. "Stop that brat!"

The Rowra blinked. Whether he would have obeyed if he had been sober, or if he had not been brooding about other races and the general unfairness of life, is an open question. He was not a bad felino-centauroid at heart. But as it was, he saw Alex running toward the ship, growled the one word *"Primate!"* to himself, and crouched for a leap.

His first mistake had been getting drunk. His second was to ignore, or be unaware of, three facts. These were, in order:

1) A Hoka, though not warlike, enjoys a roughhouse.

2) A Hoka's tubby appearance is most deceptive; he is, for instance, more than a match for any human.

3) Baloo and Bagheera did not think Shere Khan should be allowed to harm the Man-Cub.

Heragli leaped. Baloo met him in mid-air, head to head. There was a loud, hollow *thonk*, and Heragli fell into a sitting position with a dazed look on his face while Baloo did a reeling sort of off-to-Buffalo. At that moment, Bagheera entered the wars. He would have been more effective had he not religiously adhered to the principle of fighting like a black panther, scrambling onto the Rowra's back, scratching and biting.

"Ouch!" howled Heragli, regaining full consciousness. "What the sputz? Get the snrrowl off me! Leggo, you illegitimate forsaken ob-

ject of an origin which the compilers of Leviticus would not have approved! Wrowrrl!" And he made frantic efforts to reach over his shoulder.

"Striped Killer!" squeaked Bagheera joyously. "Hunter of helpless frogs! Lame Thief of the Waingunga! Take that! And that!"

"What're you talking about? Never ate a frog in m' life. Unhand me—gug!" Bagheera had wrapped both study arms around Heragli's neck and started throttling him.

At the same time Baloo recovered sufficiently to stage a frontal attack. Fortunately, being in the role of a bear, he could fight like a bear, which is to say, very much like a Hoka. Accordingly, he landed a stiff one-two on Heragli's nose and then, as the Rowra reared up, wheezing, he fell into a clinch that made his enemy's ribs creak. Breaking cleanly, he landed a couple of hard punches in the midriff of Heragli's torso, chopped him over the heart, sank his teeth into the right foreleg, was lifted off his feet by an anguished jerk, used the opportunity to deliver a double kick to the chin while flurrying a series of blows, and generally made himself useful.

"Run, Alex!" cried Tanni.

The boy paused, uncertain, as Rowra and Hokas tore up the sod a meter from him.

"Run ! Do what Mother tells you! Get help!"

Reluctantly, Alex turned and sped for the woods. Tanni felt Echpo's grasp shift as he moved behind her. When he pulled a Holman raythrower from beneath his tunic, the blood seemed to drain out of her heart.

"Believe me, dear lady, I deplore this," said the Chakban. "I had hoped to keep my weapon unknown and untouched. But we cannot risk your son's warning the authorities too soon, can we? And then there are those Hokas." He pinned her against the wall and sighted on Alex. "You *do* understand my position, don't you?" he asked anxiously.

Struggling and screaming, Tanni clawed for his eyes. The brow ridges defeated her. She saw the gun muzzle steady—

—and there was a shock that threw her from Echpo's grip and out onto the ground.

Dazed, she scrambled to her feet with a wild notion of throwing herself in the path of the beam . . . But where *was* Echpo?

The airlock seemed to hold nothing but coil upon coil of Seesis. Only gradually, as her vision cleared, did Tanni make out a contorted face among those cable-thick bights. The Chakban was scarcely able to breathe, let alone move.

"Ssssssso!" Seesis adjusted his pince-nez and regarded his prisoner censoriously. "So you lied to me. You were prepared to commit violence after all. I am shocked and grieved. I thought you shared my abhorrence of bloodshed. I see that you must be gently but firmly educated until you understand the error of your ways and repent and enter the gentle brotherhood of beings. Lie still, now, or I will break your back."

"I—" gasped Echpo. "I . . . had . . . my . . . duty—"

"And I," answered Seesis, swaying above him, "have my honor."

Alex fell into his mother's arms. She was not too full of thanksgiving to pick up the fallen gun. Across the meadow, Baloo and Bagheera stood triumphant over a semi-conscious Heragli and beamed at their snaky ally.

The Cold Lairs were taken. The Man-Cub had been rescued from Bandar-log and Lame Thief. Kaa's Hunting was finished.

The Napoleon Crime

Be it understood at the outset, the disaster was in no way the fault of Tanni Hostrup Jones. Afterward she blamed herself bitterly, but most unfairly. She was overburdened with other matters, hence unable to concentrate on this one. She had no reason whatsoever to suspect evil of Leopold Ormen; after all, he was a Dane like herself, as well as being a famous journalist. Furthermore, while Tanni was chaste, she was a full-blooded woman, her husband had been gone for days and might not return for weeks, and Ormen had a great deal of masculine charm.

Having arrived on Toka by private spacecraft and settled into the Mixumaxu Hilton, he made an appointment to see her and at the time agreed on arrived at the plenipotentiary's residence. The day was beautiful and the walk through the quaint streets a delight. Native

Hokas swarmed about, their exuberance often becoming deference when they saw the human. He smiled benignly and patted an occasional cub on the head. The adults looked just as cuddly: rather like bipedal, meter-tall teddy bears with golden fur and stubby hands, attired in a wild variety of costumes, everything from a barbarian's leather and iron to the elegant gray doublet and hose of his little companion, as well as Roman, Mandarin, cowboy, and other garb. Yet with few exceptions the squeaky voices chattered in English.

Thus, when he reached his destination, Ormen was not unduly surprised to be greeted at the door by a Hoka wearing coarse medieval-like clothes, hobnailed boots, a yellow hood, and a long white false beard tucked into a broad belt from which hung a geologist's hammer, a coil of rope, and a lantern. "Hello," the man said, and gave his name. "Mrs. Jones is expecting me."

The Hoka bowed, careful to do so in a fashion that showed he was not accustomed to bowing. "Gimli the dwarf, at your service," he replied, as gruffly as his larynx allowed. "Welcome to Rivendell. The Lady Galadriel did indeed make known to me that—Ah, ha! Hold!" Both his hands shot out and seized Ormen's left.

"What off Earth?" exclaimed the journalist.

"Begging your pardon, but that ring you're wearing. You'll have to check it before you go in."

"Why?" Ormen stared down at the gold

band and its synthetic diamond. "It's only an ornament."

"I doubt not your faith, good sir," declared Gimli, "but you may conceivably have been tricked. This *could* be the One Ring under a false seeming—you not even invisible. Can't be too careful in these darkling times, right? You'll get it back when you leave."

Ormen tried to pull free, but the native was too strong. Suppressing an oath, the visitor yielded. Gimli turned the ring over to an elderly Hoka who had shown up, also white-bearded but attired in a blue robe and pointed hat and bearing a staff. Thereafter the self-styled dwarf ceremoniously conducted Ormen through the door. The entry-room beyond had been hung with tapestries that appeared to have been very hastily woven; colored tissue glued on the windowpanes imitated stained glass, while candlelight relieved the dimness. Elsewhere the house remained a normal Terrestrial-type place, divided between living quarters and offices.

Tanni Jones received the newcomer graciously in her parlor. She was tall, blond, and comely, as was he, and eager to see anybody from the home planet. "Please sit down, Mr. Ormen," she invited. "Would you care for coffee, tea, or perhaps something alcoholic?"

"Well, I've heard about the liquor they make here, and confess to being curious," he said.

She shuddered a bit. "I don't recommend you investigate. What about a Scotch and soda?" When he accepted, she rang for a servant, who appeared with churchwarden pipe in hand and bare feet on which the hair had been combed upward. "We'll have the happy hour usual, Gamgee," she said. "*Scotch* Scotch, mind you."

The humans began to talk in earnest. "What's happening?" Ormen inquired. "I mean, well, isn't your staff acting rather oddly?"

Tanni sighed. "They've discovered *The Lord of the Rings*. I can only hope they get over it before the fashion spreads further. Not that it would upset Alex—my husband, that is, the plenipotentiary—to be hailed as the rightful King when he returns. He's used to that sort of thing, after all our years in this post. But meanwhile—oh, for example, we get visitors from other worlds, nonhumans, and many of them are important—officials of the League, representatives of firms whose cooperation we need to modernize Toka, and so on." She shuddered again. "I can just imagine the Hokas deciding some such party must be orcs or trolls or Ring-Wraiths."

"I sympathize. You inhabit a powder keg, don't you?"

"M-m, not really. The Hokas do take on any role that strikes their fancy, and act it out—live it—with an uncompromising literalmindedness. But they're not insane. They've never yet gotten violent, for instance; and they continue to work, meet their responsibilities, even if it is in some fantasy style. In fact," said Tanni anxiously, "their reputation for craziness is quite undeserved. It's going to handicap my husband on his mission. I suppose you know he's gone to Earth to negotiate an upgrading in status for Toka. If he doesn't succeed in convincing the authorities our wards are ready for that, we may never in our lifetimes see them become full members of the Interbeing League; and that is our dearest dream."

Leopold Ormen nodded. "I do know all this, Mrs. Jones, and I believe I can help." He leaned forward, though he resisted the temptation to stroke her hand. "Not that I'm an altruist. I have my own living to make, and I think there's a tremendous documentary to be done about this planet. But if it conveys the truth, in depth, to civilized viewers throughout the galaxy—yes, and readers too, because I'd also like to write a book—public opinion should change. Wouldn't that be good for your cause?"

Tanni glowed. "It certainly would!"

Ormen leaned back. She was hooked, he knew; now he must play his line so carefully that she remained unaware of the fact. "I can't do it unless I have complete freedom," he stated. "I realize your husband's duty requires him to impose various restrictions on outsiders, who might otherwise cause terrible trouble. But I hope you—in his absence, you are the acting plenipotentiary, aren't you?—I hope you'll authorize me to go anywhere, see anything and anybody, for as long as I'll need to get the whole story. I warn you, that may take quite a while, and I'll be setting my aircar down in places where the Hokas aren't accustomed to such a sight."

As said, Tanni cannot be blamed. She did not rush into her decision. In the course of the following week, she had several meetings with him, including a couple of dinners where he was a fascinating, impeccably courteous guest. She inquired among the local folk, who all spoke well of him. She studied recordings of his previous work from the data file, and found it excellent. When at last she did give him *carte blanche*, she expected to keep track of what he was doing, and call a halt if a blunder seemed imminent. Besides, Alex should be back presently, to apply the sixth sense he had perforce developed for problems abrew.

That none of these reasonable considerations worked out was simply in the nature of Hoka things.

First she was kept busy distracting the natives, lest a Tolkien craze sweep through thousands of them. That was less difficult than it might have been elsewhere on the globe. Most of the human-derived societies were still rather isolated and naive. This was a result of policy on Alex's part. Not only did he fear the unforeseeable consequences of cross-fertilization—suppose, for example, that the Vikings came into close contact with the Bedouins—but a set of ongoing, albeit uncontrolled psychohistorical experiments gave him hints about what was best for the race as a whole. Nevertheless, it did leave those cultures vulnerable to any new influence that happened by.

As the seat of the plenipotentiary and therefore, in effect, the capital city of the planet, Mixumaxu was cosmopolitan. Its residents and those of its hinterland were, so to speak, immunized. This did not mean that any individual stuck to any given role throughout his life. On the contrary, he was prone to overnight changes. But by the same token, these made no fundamental difference to him; and therefore the Jones household continued to function well in a bewildering succession of guises.

Soon after she had headed off the War of the Rings, Tanni got caught up in the *Jungle Books* affair. Since that involved beings of status, and a scandal which must not become common knowledge lest the tranquility of the galaxy be disturbed, the sequel kept her occupied for weeks. She handled her end of the business with a competence which caused the Grand Theocrat of Sanussi, in an elaborate honors ceremony years later, to award her a cast-off skin of his.

Meanwhile a cruel disappointment arrived, in the form of a letter from Alex. Complications had developed; the delegation from Kratch was, for some reason known only to their nasty little selves, using every parliamentary trick to delay the upgrading of Toka; he must stay and fight the matter through to a successful conclusion; he didn't know how long it would take; he missed her immeasurably, and enclosed one of his poems to prove it.

Tanni refrained from weeping in front of their children. She did utter a few swear words. Afterward she plunged into work. Suddenly there seemed to be a great deal of it. Information-gathering facilities were stretched thin at best, so that she was seldom fully apprised of events on other continents; but such reports as came in were increasingly ominous. They told of unrest, strange new ideas, revolutionary changes—

No wonder that she lacked time to follow what Leopold Ormen was about. Events moved far too fast. All at once she saw catastrophe looming before her. The single thing she could think to do was send a frantic, although enciphered, message to her husband; and indeed, this was the single thing she could have done.

An airbus took Alexander Jones from League headquarters in New Zealand to the spaceport on Campbell Island. There he walked past sleek, gleaming starships to the far end of the field, where sat a craft larger than most, but battered and corrosion-pocked. Its bulbous lines proclaimed it to be of nonhuman manufacture, and its registration emblem to be a tramp freighter. Beneath the name etched on the bows was a translation into the English of the spaceways: *Thousand-Year Bird*. Alex mounted the movable ramp that led to the main personnel lock and pressed the buzzer button.

A gentle, if mechanical voice sounded from the speaker grille: "Is someone present? The valve isn't secured. Come in, do, and make yourself at home."

Alex pushed on the metal. Nothing happened. "Brob, it's me, Alexander Jones," he said into the intercom. "It won't open. The valve won't, I mean."

"Oh, dear, I *am* sorry. I forgot I had left it on manual. One moment, please. I beg your pardon for the inconvenience."

Something like a minor earthquake shivered through hull and ramp. The valve swung aside, revealing an oversized airlock chamber and the being who had the strength to move so ponderous an object. "How pleasant to see you again, dear fellow," said the transponder hanging from his neck. Meanwhile his real voice, which the device rendered into frequencies a human could hear, vibrated subsonically out of his feet and up into the man's bones. "Welcome to my humble vessel. Come in, let me make you a cup of tea, tell me how I may serve you."

The 'sponder likewise converted Alex's tones into impulses Brob sensed through his skin. On their airless world, his species had never developed ears. "I've got a hell of a request to make, and you don't really know me well enough, but I'm desperate and you seem to be my only possible help."

Eyes that were soft and brown, despite their

lack of moisture, looked thirty centimeters downward to Alex's lanky height. "Sir, it has been a pleasure and an enlightenment making your acquaintance. Furthermore, I feel certain that your purpose is not selfish, but for some public good. If so, whatever small assistance I can perhaps render will earn me merit, which I sorely need. Therefore it shall be I who enter into your debt. Now do come in and tell me about this."

Brob led the way, moving gracefully despite his bulk; but then, Earth gravity was a mere one-third of his planet's. For that matter, had he been short like a Hoka, he would have been considered even more cute. He too possessed a pair of arms, his thicker than a gorilla's and terminating in enormous four-fingered hands, and a pair of stout legs, ending in feet that were a meter long and half as wide; their soles enclosed the tympani with which his race listened and spoke. The torso was so rotund as to be almost globular. The head was equally round; though it naturally lacked a nose, it had a blunt snout whose lipless mouth was shaped into a permanent smile. All in all, he suggested a harp seal puppy. Baby-blue fur covered him, save on the hands and feet; there it was white, which gave him an appearance of wearing mittens and booties. His actual clothing consisted of the 'sponder and a belt with pockets full of assorted tools.

The saloon of the ship whose owner, captain, and crew he was seemed less alien than might have been expected, considering how unlike Earth was the planet which humans called Brobdingnag. That world had begun as a body more massive than Jupiter. A nearby super-nova had blown away its gas and deposited vast quantities of heavy elements over the solidifying core. They included radioactives. Somehow life had evolved, making use of this source of energy rather than the feeble red sun. Plants concentrated isotopes which animals then ate. Brob, as Alex dubbed him for lack of ability to pronounce his real name, did not live by oxidizing organic materials like most creatures in known space, but by fissioning nuclei. His physical strength was corresponding.

The metabolism posed no hazard to anyone else. The fission process worked at a far lower level than in a powerplant, and whatever radiation it gave off was absorbed by the dense tissues around the "stomach." Brobdingnagians traveling abroad needed merely take certain precautions in disposal of their body wastes. Regardless, many beings feared and shunned them. Having delivered a cargo to Earth, Brob found himself unable to get another, and the waiting time while his broker searched for one grew lonely as well as long. Chancing to meet Alex in a Christchurch pub, where he had gone in hopes that somebody would talk to him, he was pathetically grateful when the man not only did, but pursued the acquaint-ance afterward.

For his part, Alex enjoyed Brob's tales of

distant worlds. Sometimes he grew bored, because the alien had fallen in love with Japanese culture and would drone on for hours about calligraphy, flower arranging, and other such arts. Yet even that was better than sitting around yearning for Tanni and his children, cursing the abominable Kratch, and wondering how many more weeks it would take to complete his business.

Brob did his best to bow as he gestured his visitor to sit down on a tatami mat, politely ignoring the shoes that the human had not removed. He left Alex to meditate upon a lily and a stone, placed in a bowl of water beneath a scroll depicting Mount Fuji, while he occupied himself preparing for a tea ceremony. This was necessarily modified, since as he sipped the aqueous substance, it turned to steam. Serenely, he contemplated the white clouds swirling out of his mouth, before at last he inquired what he could do for his friend.

Alex had learned not to be boorishly direct in Brob's presence. "Let me review the situation, though you do know why I'm stuck here on Earth," he said. "The Chief Cultural Commissioner had approved Toka's advancement, the vote looked like being a pure formality, and then the Kratch delegation objected. They couldn't just be voted down, because they levelled charges of misgovernment. Nothing as simple as tyranny or corruption. I could easily have disproved that. No, they claim my

entire policy has been wrong and is bound to
cause disaster."

Brob nodded gravely. "You have explained to
me," he replied; the teapot and cups trembled.
"I have admired your restraint in not dwelling upon it in conversation."

Alex shrugged. "What use would that be?
The fact is, I've often had to do things on
Toka that, well, played kind of fast and loose
with the letter of the law. I had no choice.
The Hokas are like that. You know; I've told
you a bundle about them. Ordinarily no one
sees anything wrong in a plenipotentiary exer-
cising broad discretion. After all, every planet
is unique. Nothing really counts except results,
and I pride myself that mine have been good.
But how can I argue against the claim that
I've created the *potential* for calamity?"

"I should think a look at your record, and a
modicum of common sense, would suffice to
make the legislators decide in your favor."

"Oh, yes. But you see, after they'd raised
this issue, the Kratch promptly raised a host
of others, and got mine postponed. It's blatant obstruction on their part. Most of the
delegates recognize that and are as disgusted
as I am. But the Constitution forces them to
go through the motions—and forces me to sit
idle, waiting for whatever instant it will be
that the case of Toka is opened to debate.

"It's enough to make a paranoid out of
a saint," Alex sighed. "One set of villains
after another, year after year—the Slissii, the
Pornians, the Sarennians, the Worbenites, the

Chakbans—my wife wrote me about those—conspiring and conniving. I've really begun to wonder if some evil masterminds aren't at work behind the scenes, and I wouldn't be surprised but what they're Kratch." He sighed again. "It's either believe that, or else believe we're only characters in a series of stories being written by a couple of hacks who need the money."

"It may be sheer accident," Brob suggested. "Mortal fallibility. There is a great deal of wisdom in the universe; unfortunately, it is divided up among individuals."

Alex ran a hand through his already rumpled brown hair. His snub-nosed countenance grew stark. "Okay," he said, "what I've come to you about is a . . . a sort of dreadful climax. I've received a letter from my wife and—Toka really is about to explode. I've got to get back at once and see if I can do anything to save the situation."

"Well, yes, I should imagine that that would be indicated," Brob murmured and rumbled. "Can you describe the problem a little more fully?"

Alex pulled the letter out of his tunic. "She sent it by message torpedo; it's that urgent. It's coded, too, but by now the words are burned into my brain. Let me give you a sample." He read aloud:

" 'Somehow, our policy of keeping the different Hoka societies relatively isolated has broken down. Suddenly, they had been introduced to concepts of each other. And this hasn't been in the casual way of individuals traveling around, like that sweet little Viking you met when you'd been press-ganged onto that eighteenth-century British frigate. We've always allowed for that degree of contact. No, what's happened this time must have been deliberately caused. Besides, ideas totally new to the planet, dangerous ideas, have been appearing. I've had agents in the field collecting books, video tapes—but the damage has already been done, and the Hokas themselves don't know or care how it happened. A fire like that is fatally easy to start; then it spreads of itself.

" 'For instance, right on the plains of this continent, the Wild West has been introduced to the biography of Genghis Khan. Of course the cowboys promptly went overboard for being ferocious Mongols—'Er, Tanni ordinarily handles her figures of speech better than that; but anyway—'So far it's been harmless. The Mongols ride around to every cow town demanding it surrender to the will of the Kha Khan, and explaining that they don't stutter but "Kha Khan" really is his title. The town is always happy to yield, because they make this the occasion of a drunken party. As one mayor said to me when I flew there to question him, it's better to bottle a place than sack it. But the potential is terrifying, because the cowboys out Montana way have decided they're European knights who must resist any heathen who invade their country.

" 'And the Russian Hokas are no longer content to sit around strumming balalaikas and singing sad songs; they have elected a Czar and babble about the Third Rome. Over in the United States, Abolitionists are feverishly looking for slaves to set free—and beginning to get volunteer Uncle Tom types—while the Virginia Gentlemen talk of secession. In the South Sea, a King Kamehameha has appeared, and war clubs are replacing ukuleles, and I'm afraid they'll see use. It goes on and on around the globe, this sort of dangerous nonsense.

" 'What frightens me worst, and causes me to write this, is Napoleon.' " Alex cleared his throat. "You realize, Brob, that a Hoka can be perfectly sane and still claim he is Napoleon. Um-m.... 'He has displaced the King of France. He is organizing and equipping his Grand Army. Even after my experience of Hoka energy and enthusiasm, I am surprised at how fast the workshops in their country are producing weapons.

" 'Inevitably, those eighteenth-century British have gotten alarmed and are arming too. Their island is right across a strait from that continent, you remember. I might have been able to calm them down, except that lengthy biographies of humans who lived in that period have been circulating to inflame their imaginations. I was in London, trying to argue them out of it, and threatening to expose them to the ridicule of the galaxy. I couldn't think what else to do. The Hoka who calls himself the Duke of Wellington drew himself up to his full height, fixed me with a steely eye, and barked, "Publish and be damned!"

" 'Oh, darling, I'm afraid! I think these play-acting prophecies of wars to come will soon fulfill themselves. And once Hokas actually start getting maimed and killed—well, I believe you'll agree that they'll go berserk, as bad as ever our species was in the past, and the whole planet will be drenched in blood.

" 'Alex, could you possibly return?' "

The man's voice broke. He stuffed the letter back into his pocket and dabbed at his eyes. "You see I've got to go," he said.

"Do you expect that you can accomplish anything?" Brob asked, as softly as he was able.

Alex gulped. "I've got to try."

"But you are compelled to remain here on Earth, waiting for the unpredictable moment at which you will be called upon to justify your actions as plenipotentiary and urge the upgrading of your wards."

"That's no good if meanwhile everything else I'm responsible for goes down the drain. In fact, a horror like that would throw the whole system of guidance for backward worlds into question. It could open the way for old-fashioned imperialism and exploitation of them."

"If you departed for Toka," Brob said, "the Kratch would doubtless seize that opportunity to bring up the matter of your stewardship—when you are not present to defend yourself—and win custody of the planet for one of their own, who could then work toward the end of discrediting the present protective laws, as you suggest." He made a sign. "If this hypothesis maligns the motives of the Kratch, I apologize and abase myself."

"You needn't, I'm sure." Alex leaned forward. His index finger prodded Brob's mountainous chest. "I've been collecting information about them. Their government is totalitarian, and has expansionist ambitions. It's been engaged in all sorts of shenanigans—which have been hushed up by nice-nelly types in the League who hope that if you ignore a villain he'll go away. This whole thing on Toka can't be simple coincidence. It's too well orchestrated. The likelihood of war arises precisely when I can't be on hand—Do you see?"

"What then do you propose?" asked Brob, calm as ever.

"Why, this," Alex said. "Look. Toka's a backwater. No passenger liners call there. If I left on my official ship, it would be known; I need clearance for departure, and the Kratch must have somebody keeping watch on this port. They'd immediately move to get their accusations onto the floor, and probably have their agents do their best to hasten the debacle on Toka. But if they don't *know* I've gone—if they assume I'm hanging around waiting and drinking too much as I have been— they'll let matters continue to ripen while they continue to stall. And maybe I can do something about the whole miserable affair. Do you see?"

Brob nodded. "I believe I do," he answered. "You wish me to furnish clandestine transportation."

"I don't know who else can," Alex pleaded. "As for payment, well, I have discretionary funds in my exchequer, and if I can get this mess straightened out—"

Brob swept an arm in a grand gesture which smashed the tea table. "Oh, dear," he murmured; and then, almost briskly: "Say no more. We need not discuss crass cash. I will tell my broker that I have lost patience and am departing empty. Your task will be to smuggle yourself and your rations aboard. Do you not prefer ham sandwiches?"

Despite its down-at-heels appearance, the *Thousand-Year Bird* was a speedster, powerplant equal to a dreadnaught's and superlight drive as finely tuned as an express courier's. It made the passage from Sol to Brackney's Star in scarcely more than a week. Alex supposed that Brobdingnagians had an innate talent for that kind of engineering; or maybe it was just that they could work on a nuclear reactor as casually as a human could tinker with an aircar engine, and thus acquired a knack for it.

Quite aside from the crisis, Alex had reason to be glad of such a high pseudovelocity. It wasn't so much that Brob, profusely apologizing, kept the artificial gravity at that of his home world. His health required a spell of this, in between his long stay on Earth and his prospective stay on Toka. Given a daily dose of baryol, Alex could tolerate the condition for a while, though soon his lean frame grew stiff and sore under its weight of 240 kilos and he spent most of the time stretched out on an enormous bunk. The real trouble was that Brob, having little else to do under way, spent most of same time keeping him company and trying to cheer him up; and Brob's bedside manner left something to be desired.

The alien's intentions were of the kindliest. His race had no natural enemies even on its own planet; if he chose, he could have pulled apart the collapsed metal armor of a warcraft, rather like a man ripping a newsfax sheet in half. Hence he had no reason not to be full of love for all life forms, and—while he knew from experience that it was not always true—his tendency was to assume that all of them felt likewise.

After a few sermons on the moral necessity of giving the Kratch the benefit of the doubt, since they were probably only misguided, Alex lost his temper. "You'll find out different when they bring an end to a hundred years of peace!" he yelled. "Let me alone about it, will you?"

An apologetic quiver went through the hull. "Forgive me," Brob said. "I am sorry. I didn't mean to raise thoughts you must find painful. Shall we discuss flower arrangements?"

"Oh, no, not that again! Tell me about some more of your adventures."

The 'sponder burbled, which perhaps corresponded to a sigh. "Actually, I have had few. For the most part I have simply plodded among the stars, returning home to my little wife and our young ones, where we cultivate our garden and engage in various activities for civic betterment. Of course, I have seen remarkable sights on my travels, but you don't appreciate how outstanding among them are those of Earth. Why, in Kyoto I found a garden which absolutely inspired me. I am certain my wife will agree that we must remodel ours along similar lines. And an arrangement of our very own glowbranch, ion weed, and lightning blossoms would—" Brob was off afresh on his favorite subject.

Alex composed his soul in patience. The Hokas had given him plenty of practice at that.

The ship set down on Mixumaxu spaceport, Brob turned off the interior fields, and suddenly Alex was under blessed Terrestrial-like weight again. Whooping, he sprang from his bunk, landed on the deck, and collapsed as if his legs had turned to boiled spaghetti.

"Dear me," said his companion. "Your system must be more exhausted than we realized. How I regret the necessity I was under. Let me offer you assistance." Reaching down, he took a fold of the man's tunic between thumb and forefinger, lifted him daintily, and bore him off to the airlock, not noticing that Alex's feet dangled several centimeters in the air.

After taking parking orbit around the planet,

he had radioed for permission to land. He had mentioned that the plenipotentiary was aboard, but forgotten to say anything about himself; and nobody on Toka had heard about his race, whose trade lanes did not bring them into this sector. Thus the ground crew who had brought the ramp, and Tanni who had sped from her home, were treated to the sight of their man feebly asprawl in the grip of a leering, blue-furred ogre.

A native security guard whipped out a pistol. "Hold still, sir!" he squeaked. "I'll kill that monster for you."

"No, no, don't shoot," Alex managed to croak.

"Why not?"

"Well, in the first place," said Alex, making his tone as reasonable as possible under the circumstances, "he wouldn't notice. But mainly, he's a good person, and—and—Hi, there, honey."

The ramp, which had not been constructed for the likes of Brob, shivered and buckled as he descended, but somehow he made it safely. Meanwhile Alex thought the poison must have spread far and deep, if a Hoka—in sophisticated Mixumaxu, at that—was so quick to resort to a lethal weapon.

Tanni's passionate embrace proved remarkably restorative. He wished they could go home, just the two of them, at once, before the children got back from school. However, politeness required that they invite Brob to come along, and when they were at the house, Alex's fears resurged and he demanded an account of the latest developments.

Woe clouded Tanni's loveliness. "Worse every day," she answered. "Especially in Europe—our Europe, I mean," she added to Brob, "though don't confuse it with that Europe that the ex-cowboys in what used to be Montana have—Never mind." She drew breath and started over:

"Napoleon's filled the French Hokas with dreams of *la gloire*, and the German Hokas are flocking to become his grenadiers—except in Prussia, where I've heard about a General Blücher—and three days ago, the Grand Army invaded Spain. You see, Napoleon wants to give the Spanish throne to his cousin Claud. That's caused the British Hokas—the British circa 1800 A.D., that is—thank God, so far the Victorian British on their own island have kept their senses, maybe because of Sherlock Holmes—anyway, yesterday they declared war, and are raising a fleet and an army of their own for a Peninsular campaign. And we won't even be able to handle the matter discreetly. I got hold of Leopold Ormen by phone and begged him to clear his stories with me, but he refused—insisted on his right of a free press, and in such a gloating way, too. . . . I'd taken him for a nice man, but—" Her voice broke. She huddled down in her chair and covered her face.

"Leopold Ormen? The journalist?" inquired Alex. "What's this?"

Tanni explained, adding that the man had since gone elsewhere, quite out of contact.

Alex cursed. "As if we didn't have troubles enough!" Suspicion struck fangs into his spirit. "Could his presence here be simple coincidence? I wonder. I wonder very much."

"Do you imply that Mr. Ormen may have stirred up this imbroglio?" asked Brob, appalled. "If so, and if you are correct, I fear he is no gentlebeing."

Alex sprang from his seat and paced. "Well, he can scarcely have accomplished everything alone," he thought aloud. "But he can sure have helped a lot to get it started, flitting freely around with the prestige of being a human, and that glib manner I recall from his broadcasts. . . . Don't cry, darling."

"I shan't," Brob said. "My species does not produce tears. However, I am deeply moved by your expression of affection."

Tanni had not begun sobbing. That was not her way. Grimly, she raised her glance and said, "Okay, he tricked me. At least, we've sufficient grounds for suspicion to order his arrest. Though he has his own flyer and could be anywhere on the planet."

Alex continued to prowl the carpet. "I doubt that that would be any use at this stage," he responded. "Arresting him, I mean. Unless we had absolute proof that he was engaged in subversion, which we don't, we'd lay ourselves open to countercharges of suppression. Besides, our first duty is not to save our reputations, but to prevent bloodshed."

He struck fist in palm, again and again. "How *could* matters have gotten so out of hand, so fast?" he wondered. "Even for Hokas, this is extreme, and it's happened damn near overnight. Around the globe, too, you tell me; the Napoleon business is just the most immediate danger. Somebody, some group, must be at work, propagandizing, offering evil advice. They wouldn't have to be humans, either. Hokas would be ready to believe whatever they heard from members of any technologically advanced society. In fact, humans have gotten to be rather old hat. Somebody different, exotic, would have more glamour, and find it easier to mislead them."

"Yes, I've thought along the same lines, dear," Tanni said. "Naturally, I forbade the French to mobilize, but the only reply I got was something about the Old Guard dies, it does not surrender. The British—well, they ignored my countermanding of their declaration of war, but I don't think they have been directly subverted. They're simply reacting as one would expect them to."

Alex nodded. "That sounds likely. The enemy can't have agents everywhere. That'd be too conspicuous, and give too many chances for something to go wrong. A few operatives, in key areas, are better."

He stopped in midstride, tugged his chin, rumpled his hair, and decided: "Britain is the place to start, then. I'm off to see what I can do. After all, I am their plenipotentiary, whom they've known for years, and if I appear in person, they'll at least listen to me."

"Shall I accompany you?" offered Brob. "On Toka I am, if not glamorous, surely exotic. Thus my presence may lend weight."

"It will that!" Alex agreed. He supposed his aircar could lift the other being.

Numerous Georgian houses graced the city renamed London. Though the Hokas could not afford to replace every older building at once, they had decorated many a wall with fake pilasters, put dummy dormers onto round roofs, and cut fanlights into doors. Tophatted, tailcoated Regency bucks swaggered through the streets, escorting ladies in muslin; seeing Alex and Brob, such males would raise their quizzing glasses for a closer look. Inspired by Hogarth, the commoners who swarmed about were more vocal at sight of the newcomers. Luckily, the dinosaurian animals hitched to wagons and carriages were not as excitable as Terrestrial horses. In general, this place was more safe and sanitary than its model had been; Alex had managed to bring that about in every society that his wards adopted.

Thus far. Today he saw a high proportion of redcoated soldiers who shouldered muskets with bayonets attached. He overheard a plaintive voice through a tavern window: "Please, matey, do resist us like a good lad. 'Ow can we be a proper press gang h'if h'everybody *volunteers*?"

Proceeding afoot, since Brob would have

190

broken the axles of any local vehicle, Alex and his companion reached Whitehall. There a guard of Royal Marines saluted and led them to the First Lord of the Admiralty. The man had called ahead for this appointment; even the most archaic-minded Hokas maintained essential modern equipment in their more important offices, although in the present case the visiphone was disguised as a Chippendale cabinet. The native behind the desk rose. He had attired his portly form in brown smallclothes and set a wig on his head. It didn't fit well, and rather distracted from the fine old-world courtesy of his bow, by slipping down over his muzzle.

"A pleasure to meet you again, my dear fellow, 'pon my word it is," he said in calm, clipped accents while he readjusted the wig. "And to make your acquaintance, sir," he added to Brob, "as I trust I shall have the honor of doing. Be seated and take refreshment." He tinkled a bell. The staff were prepared, for a liveried servant entered immediately, bearing a tray with three glasses and a dusty bottle. "Fine port, this, if I do say so myself." Indignantly: "To think that Boney would cut us off from the source of supply! Infernal bounder, eh, what? Well, damme, he'll whistle a different tune, and out of a dry throat, when we've put him on St. Helena."

Alex settled down and took a cautious sip from his goblet. The drink was the same fiery distillation that was known as claret, sherry, brandy, rum, whisky, or whatever else a role might call for. "I am afraid, Lord Oakheart, that Bonaparte has no intention of going to St. Helena," he replied. "Instead—" He broke off, because the Hoka's jaw had dropped. Turning about to see what was wrong, he spied Brob. The giant spacefarer, careful to remain standing, had politely swallowed the drink given him. Blue flames gushed out of his mouth.

"Er, this is my associate, from Brobdingnag," Alex explained.

"From where?" asked Oakheart. "I mean to say, that Swift chap does have several interesting ideas, but I wasn't aware anybody had put 'em into effect . . . yet." Recovering his British aplomb, he took a pinch of snuff.

Alex braced himself. "Milord," he said, "you know why we've come. Armed conflict cannot be allowed. The differences between the governments of His Majesty and the Emperor shall have to be negotiated peacefully. To that end, my good offices are available, and I must insist they be accepted. The first step is for you people to take, namely, cancelling your expedition to Spain."

"Impossible, sir, impossible," huffed the Hoka. "Lord Nelson sails from Plymouth tomorrow. True, at present he has only the Home Fleet under his command, but dispatches are on their way to the colonies, summoning all our strength afloat to join him at Trafalgar. How can we stop 'em, eh? No, the British Lion is off to crush the knavish Frogs."

Alex thought fast. A leaderless armada, mill-ing about, would have still more potential for causing disaster than one which was assembled under its respected admiral. "Wait a minute," he said. "It'll take two or three weeks for those windjammers to reach the rendezvous, whereas Spain's only two or three days' sail from here. Why is Nelson leaving this early?"

Oakheart confirmed his guess: "A reconnaissance, sir, a reconnaissance in force, to gather intelligence on the enemy's movements and chivvy him wherever he shows his cowardly face with fewer ships than ours."

"In that case, suppose I ride along. I could, well, maybe give Lord Nelson some helpful advice. More importantly, being on the scene, I could attempt to open negotiations with the French."

Oakheart frowned. "Most irregular. Danger of violation of the Absolutely Extreme Secrets Act. I am afraid I cannot countenance—"

Alex had learned how to turn Hoka logic against itself. "See here, milord, I am the accredited representative of a sovereign state with which your own has treaties and trade relations. I am sure His Majesty's government will accord me the usual diplomatic courtesies."

"Well . . . ah . . . but if you must talk to that Bonaparte rascal, why don't you simply fly to his camp, eh?"

Alex stiffened and replied coldly: "Sir, I am shocked to hear you propose that His Majesty's government should have no part in a vital proceeding like this."

Oakheart capitulated. "I beg your pardon,

sir! No such intention, I assure you. Roger me
if there was. Here, I'll give you a letter of
introduction to the admiral, in my own hand,
by Jove!" He reached for a goosequill, imported
at considerable expense from Earth. As he
wrote, he grew visibly more and more eager.
Alex wished he could see what was going down
on the paper, but no gentleman would read
someone else's mail.

The human had excellent reasons—he hoped
—for taking this course. While the Hoka Napoleon himself was doubtless well-intentioned,
whatever persons had inflated his vainglory
until he was red for war were, just as doubtless, not. They would be prepared for the contingency of a direct approach by a League
authority. A blaster could shoot his aircar
down as it neared, or he could be assassi-
nated or kidnapped after he landed, and the
Hokas led to believe he had been the victim
of a tragic accident.

Traveling with Nelson, he had a better
chance of getting to the Emperor, unbeknownst
to the conspirators. Whether or not he succeeded in that, he expected to gather more
information about how matters actually stood
than he could in any other fashion.

Tanni would never let him take the risk. If
nothing else, she'd fly out in her own car and
snatch him right off the ship. Reluctantly, he
decided to tell her, when he phoned, that he
was engaged in delicate business which would
keep him away for an indefinite time.

* * *

Since their ancient Slissii rivals departed, Hokas had had no need of military or naval forces, except to provide colorful uniforms and ceremonies. Hence the Home Fleet gathered at Plymouth was unimpressive. There were about a dozen Coast Guard cutters, hitherto employed in marine rescue work. There were half as many commandeered merchant ships, though these, being squareriggers of the Regency period, naturally bore cannon. There were three minor warcraft, the pinnace *Fore*, the bark *Umbrageous*, and the frigate *Falcon*. And finally there was a line-of-battle ship, the admiral's pennant at its masthead and the name *Victory* on its bows.

Leaving Brob ashore, lest the gangplank break beneath him, Alex boarded the latter. Two sailors who noticed him whipped fifes out of their jackets and played a tune, as befitted a visitor of his rank. This caused crewmen elsewhere on deck to break into a hornpipe. A Hoka in blue coat and cocked hat, telescope tucked beneath his left arm, hurried across the tarry-smelling planks.

"Welcome, Your Excellency, welcome," he said, and gave Alex a firm handshake. "Bligh's the name, Captain William Bligh, sir, at your service."

"What? I thought—"

"Well, H.M.S. *Bounty* is being careened, and besides, Lord Nelson required a sterner master in wartime than Captain Cook. Aye, a great seaman, Cook, but far too easy with the cat. What can I do for Your Excellency?"

Alex realized that a fleet admiral would not occupy himself with the ordinary duties of a skipper on his flagship. "I must see His Lordship. I have an important message for him."

Bligh looked embarrassed. He shuffled his feet. "His Lordship is resting in his stateroom, sir. Indisposed. Frail health, you know, after the rigors of Egypt."

Alex knew full well. Horatio Lord Nelson's public appearances were few and short. The nuisance of having to wear an eyepatch and keep his right arm inside his coat was too much.

Bligh recovered his spirit. He lowered his voice. "Although I'd say, myself, Lady Hamilton's had a bit to do with his weariness. *You* understand, sir." He gave Alex a wink, a leer, and a nudge in the ribs that sent the human staggering.

Instantly contrite, he offered to convey the letter. Alex gave him the sealed envelope, wishing again that he knew just what Oakheart had written. Hoka helpfulness often took strange forms. Bligh trotted aft. Alex spent the time arranging for his luggage to be fetched from his aircar. He saw Brob standing near it on the dock, surrounded by curious townsfolk, and wondered how he could do the same for his friend.

Bligh returned, twice as excited as before. "We shall have the honor of dining with His Lordship this evening," he announced. "Meanwhile, the squadron must be off on the afternoon tide. But we've time for a tot of rum in my cabin, Commodore, to welcome you into our company."

"Commodore? Huh?" Alex asked.

Bligh winked anew, though he kept his thumb to himself and, instead, took the man's elbow. "Ah, yes, I know full well. Ashore, the walls have ears. Mustn't let the Frenchies learn Commodore Hornblower is on a secret mission in disguise, damme, no. When we're safe at sea, I'll inform the men, by your leave, sir. Brace 'em up for certain, the news will, scurvy lot though they be." Walking along, he shrilled right and left at the crew: "Avast, ye lubbers! Look lively there! Flogging's too good for the likes o' ye! Keelhauling, aye, scuttle my bones if I don't keelhaul the first mutinous dog who soldiers on the job! Marines excepted, of course," he added more quietly.

In his quarters he poured, proposed the health of the King and the damnation of Boney, and fell into a long jeremiad about his lack of able officers. "The weak, piping times of peace, that's what's done it, Commodore." Alex listened with half an ear. If Oakheart's fantasy had appointed him Hornblower, maybe he could turn the situation to his advantage. Hornblower certainly rated more respect from Hoka mariners than any mere plenipotentiary—

A knock sounded on the door. "Come in, if ye've proper business," Bligh barked. "If not, beware! That's all I say, beware."

The door opened. A sailor in the usual striped shirt, bell-bottomed trousers, and straw hat saluted. A truncheon hung from his belt. "Bosun Bush, sir, press gang, reporting," he said. "We've caught us a big 'un. Does the captain want to see him?"

"Aye, what else?" Bligh snapped. "Got to set these pressed men right from the start, eh, Commo—eh, Your Excellency?"

The boatswain beckoned. Flanked by a couple of redcoated marines, Brob's enormous form made the deck creak and tremble as he approached. "What the hell?" burst from Alex. "How did they ever get you aboard?"

"They rigged a derrick," Brob answered. "Most kind of them, no? I had not even requested it when suddenly there they were, instructing me in what to do."

"Stout fella, this, hey, sir?" beamed the boatswain.

Captain Bligh peered dubiously at the acquisition. "He does look strong—" His ebullience returned to him. "Nevertheless, he'll soon find that aboard a King's ship is no life of ease." To Brob: "You'll work 'round the clock, me hearty, swab the planks, climb the ratlines, fist canvas along with the rest of 'em, or you'll hang from a yardarm. D'ye understand?"

Alex had a horrible vision of what would happen to the *Victory* if Brob tried to climb its rigging. His memory came to the rescue. Once he too had been impressed onto a ship out of this very England.

"Here's the first mate you said you lack, Captain Bligh," he declared in haste.

"What?" The skipper blinked at him.

"Pressed man always appointed first mate," said Alex, "in spite of his well-known sympathy for the crew."

"Of course, sir, of course," Bush chimed in happily.

"Well—" Bligh scratched his head. "Far be it from a simple old seaman like me to question the wisdom of Commodore Hornblower—"

"Commodore Hornblower!" The boatswain's eyes grew large. He tugged his forelock, or rather the fur where a human would have had a forelock. "Begging your pardon, sir, I didn't recognize you, but that's a clever disguise you're wearing, shiver me timbers if it ain't."

Bristling, Bligh turned his attention to Brob. "Well?" he snarled. "What're you waiting for, Mr. Christian? Turn out the crew. Put 'em to work like a proper bucko mate. We've the tide to make, and a fair wind for Spain."

"But, but I don't know how," Brob stammered.

"Don't try to cozen me with your sly ways, Fletcher Christian!" Bligh shouted. "Out on deck with you and get us moving!"

"Excuse me," Alex said. "I know this man of old, Captain. I can explain." He stepped forth, drew Brob aside, and whispered:

"Listen, this is typical Hoka dramatics. The crew are perfectly competent. They don't expect anything but a show out of the officers, as far as actual seamanship goes. You need only stand around, look impressive, and issue an occasional order—any order that comes to mind. They'll interpret it as being a command to do the right thing. Meanwhile I'll handle the details for both of us." Luckily, he reflected, that need not include rations. He could eat Tokan food, though it was preferable to supplement it with a few Terrestrial vitamin pills from his kit. He always carried some on his person. Brob had eaten before they left Mixumaxu, and one of his nuclear meals kept him fueled for weeks.

Bemused, the alien wandered off after Bosun Bush, rather like an ocean liner behind a small tugboat. Alex was taken to a vacant cabin and installed. It was reasonably comfortable, except that a human given a Hoka bed must sleep sitting up. One by one, the ships warped from the docks, set sail, and caught the breeze. When Alex re-emerged, *Victory* was rolling along over chill greenish waters, under a cloud of canvas like those that elsewhere covered the sea. Air sang in the rigging and carried a tang of salt. Crewmen went about their tasks—which included, ominously, the polishing of cannon as heavy as Brob himself—or, off watch, sat around telling each other how French blood would redden the ocean. Land was already low on the northern horizon.

Alex didn't stay topside long. He had had a difficult time of late, and faced a dinner with Lord Nelson, Captain Bligh, and heaven knew who else, in his role as Hornblower. Let him get some rest while he was able.

*   *   *

Shouts, trumpet calls, drumbeats, the thud of running feet roused him from an uneasy night's sleep. He stumbled forth in his pajamas. Pandemonium reigned, Hokas scurrying everywhere to and fro. Aloft, a lookout cried, "Thar she blows—I mean to say, Frogs ahead, two p'ints t' starboard!"

"Stand by to engage!" yelled Captain Bligh from the quarterdeck.

Alex scrambled up the ladder to join him. Nelson was there already, the empty sleeve of his dressing gown aflap in the wind, a telescope clapped to his patchless eye. "We've the weather gauge of them," he said. "They'll not escape us, I trow. Run up the signal flags: England expects every man will do his duty."

Aghast, Alex stared forward, past the bowsprit and across the whitecaps. Dawnlight showed him three large sailing vessels on the rim of sight. Despite the distance, he identified the Tricolor proudly flying at each staff. Louis XIV had built a navy too. (The Hoka France had never had a Revolution, merely an annual Bastille Day fête. At the most recent of these, Napoleon had taken advantage of the usual chaos to depose the king, who cooperated because it would be more fun being a field marshal. The excitement delighted the whole nation and charged it with enthusiasm. Only in Africa was this ignored, the Foreign Legion preferring to stay in its romantic, if desolate, outposts.)

"No danger of their escape, milord." Bligh

rubbed his hands. "See, they're coming about. They mean to meet us. We outnumber 'em, aye, but those are three capital ships. Ah, a jolly little fight it'll be."

Down on the main deck, and on the gun decks below, sailors were readying their armament. The sardonic old prayer drifted thence to Alex's ears: "For that which we are about to receive, Lord, make us duly grateful." Marine sharpshooters swarmed into the masts. He shuddered. Like children at play, the Hokas had no idea what shot and shell would inflict on them. They would find out, once the broadsides began, but then it would be too late. Nor would they recoil. He knew well how much courage dwelt in them.

Feeling ill, he mumbled, "Admiral, wouldn't it be best if we—er—avoided commitment in favor of proceeding on our mission? Preserve the King's property, you know."

Nelson was shocked. "Commodore Hornblower! Do you imagine British seamen would turn tail like a ... like a ... like a crew of tailturners? Egad, no! Britannia rules the waves! Westminster Abbey or victory!"

Captain Bligh smiled. "I'm sure the Commodore is no craven, but has some ruse in mind," he said cunningly. "What is it, sir?"

"I—well, I—" Desperate, Alex looked downward from the rail which his white-knuckled hands gripped. Brob stood like a rock in a surf of Hokas. "Can you do anything, anything at all?" the human wailed to him.

"As a matter of fact," Brob responded

diffidently, "I believe I may see a perhaps useful course of action."

"Then for mercy's sake, *do* it! Though ... we can't take French lives either, do you realize?"

"I would never dream of it." Brob fanned himself, as if the very thought made him feel faint. "You shall have to lower me over the side." He looked around him. "Possibly with one of those—er—spars to keep me afloat."

"Do you hear that?" Alex exclaimed to Nelson and Bligh. "Brob—uh, Mr. Christian can save the day." They stared blankly at him. He saw he must give them an impression of total calm, complete mastery of the situation. Somehow, he grinned and winked. "Gentlemen, I do indeed have a ruse, but there isn't time now to explain it. Please ready a cargo boom and drop the mate overboard."

Nelson grew distressed. "I do not recall, sir, that any precedent exists in the annals of war for jettisoning the mate. If we should be defeated, it would count heavily against us at our courts martial."

Bligh was quicker-witted. "Not if he's mutinied," he said. "Do you follow me, Christian, you treacherous scoundrel? Don't just stand there. Do something mutinous."

"Well, er—" With a mighty effort, against his every inclination, Brob raised a cable-thick middle finger in the air. "Up yours, sir. A rusty grapnel, sir, sideways. I do require a grapnel."

"Ah, hah! D'ye hear what he was plotting?

Next thing we knew, we'd be adrift in an open boat 4000 miles from Timor. Overboard he goes!" bellowed Bligh in his shrill soprano.

A work detail was promptly organized. To the sound of a lusty chanty, Brob, a spar firmly lashed to his massive body and carrying his implement, went on high, swung above the gunwale, and dropped into the waves. An enormous splash followed. Fearful of the outcome, yet intensely curious himself, Alex watched his friend swim off to meet the French.

They were still well out of gunshot range. Windjammers can't maneuver fast. The sight of the monster nearing them alarmed the crews, who opened fire on him. Two of the cannonballs struck, but bounced harmlessly off.

Coming to the nearest vessel, Brob trod water while he whirled his hook at the end of a long chain. He let fly. It bit hard into a mast and snugged itself against a yard. Brob dived and began to haul. Drawn by the chain, the ship canted over—and over—and over—The sea rushed in through gunports and hatches.

Brob came back to the surface. A deft yank on the chain dislodged the grapnel and brought it to him again, along with a portion of the mast that he had snapped across. The warcraft wallowed low. It was not sinking, quite, and nobody had been hurt, but its powder was drenched, leaving it helpless.

Brob gave a similar treatment to the next.

The third showed a clean pair of heels, followed by hoots of British derision.

Brob returned to the *Victory*, where his sailors winched him on deck to the tune of "Way, hey, and up he rises, ear-lie in the morning." Lord Nelson magnanimously issued him a pardon for his insubordinate conduct and Captain Bligh ordered an extra ration of grog for everybody.

Indeed, beneath their boasting, the Hokas seemed glad to have avoided combat. That gave Alex a faint hope.

Whether or not the entire naval strength available to France in these parts at this time had been routed, none was on hand when the flotilla from England dropped anchor two days afterward. Sunset light streamed over a hush broken only by the mildest of breezes and the squeals of leathery-winged seafowl. The bay here was wide and calm. Above it loomed the Iberian peninsula. Like its namesake on Earth, this land was rugged, though lushly green. A village, whitewashed walls and red tile roofs, nestled behind a wharf where fishing boats lay moored.

Also red were the coats of marines ashore. They had occupied the place as a precaution against anyone going off to inform the enemy of their arrival. It turned out that there was no danger of that. These isolated local folk were unconcerned about politics. Rather, they were overjoyed to have another set of foreign visitors. They had already seen Napoleon's Grand Army pass through.

Indeed, that host was encamped about ten kilometers off, beyond a high ridge to the southeast, alongside a river which emptied into the bay. Alex supposed the Emperor had chosen that site in order to be safe from surprise attack and bombardment out of the sea. He saw the smoke of campfires drift above trees, into the cool evening air.

Standing on the quarterdeck between Nelson and Bligh, he said fervently, "Gentlemen, I thank you for your cooperation in this secret mission of mine. Tonight I'll go ashore, alone, to, er, get the cut of the Frenchman's jib. Kindly remain while I'm gone, and please refrain from any untoward action that might warn him."

His plan was to steal into yonder camp, find Napoleon, identify himself, and demand a ceasefire (not that firing had begun, except for target practice, but the principle was the same). It should be less risky than an outsider would think. Hokas would scarcely shoot at a human, especially one whom various among them would recognize as the plenipotentiary. Instead, they would take him to their leader, who if nothing else would respect his person and let him go after they had talked.

This was the more likely because he had had the sailmaker sew him an impressive set of clothes. Gold braid covered his tunic, gold stripes went down his trousers, his boots bore spurs and his belt a saber. From the cocked hat on his head blossomed fake ostrich plumes. From his shoulders, unfastened, swung a coat reaching halfway down his calves, whose elbow-deep pockets sported huge brass buttons. Borrowed medals jingled across his left breast.

The main hazard was that the subversives would discover his presence before he had had his meeting. To minimize this chance, he meant to sneak as far as he could.

He might actually make it undetected to the Emperor's tent. On such short notice as they had had, even fast-learning Hokas could not have developed a very effective military tradition. Sentries would tend to doze at their posts, or join each other for a swig of *ordinaire* and a conversation about the exploits of Brigadier Gerard.

Nelson frowned around his eyepatch. "Chancy," he said. "Were it anybody but you, milord, I'd forbid it, I would. Still, I expect Your Grace knows what he's about."

"My Grace?" Alex asked, bewildered. "But I haven't been made a lord yet—that is, I'm plain Commodore Hornblower—" Seeing the look on the two furry faces, he gulped. "I am. Am I not?"

Captain Bligh chuckled. "Ah, milord, you're more than the bluff soldier they think of when they say 'Wellington.' That's clear. You couldn't have routed 'em as you did—as you're going to do, here in the Peninsula and so on till Waterloo—you couldn't do that if your mind weren't shrewd."

Admiration shone in Nelson's eyes. "I'll wager the playing fields of Eton had somewhat to do with that," he said. "Have no fears, Your Grace. Your secret is safe with us, until you've completed your task of gathering intelligence and are ready to take command of your troops."

"Scum of the earth, they are," Bligh muttered. "Just like my sailors. But we'll show those Frenchies what Britons are worth, eh, milord?"

Alex clutched his temples. "Omigawd, no!" He stifled further groans. Whether Oakheart had included the assertion in his letter, or whether these officers had concluded on their own account, now that he was going ashore in his gaudy uniform, that he must really be the Duke of Wellington, traveling under the alias of Horatio Hornblower—did it make any difference?

To be sure, somewhere in England a Hoka bore the same name. Tanni had mentioned him. That mattered naught, in his absence, to the elastic imaginations of the natives.

Alex struggled to remember something, anything, concerning the original Wellington. Little came to him. He had only read casually about the Napoleonic period, never studied it, for it was not an era whose re-enactment he would have allowed on Toka, if he had had any say in the matter. At one time, Alex recalled, somebody had tried to blackmail the great man, threatening to publish an account of his involvement with a woman not his wife. Drawing himself up to his full height and fixing the blackmailer with a steely eye, the

Iron Duke had snapped, "Publish and be damned!" It seemed rather a useless piece of information now, especially for a happily married man who cherished no desire for illicit affairs.

Alex blanched at the prospect of being swept along by events until he in fact commanded the British army in outright combat. That would certainly put an end to his career, and earn him a long prison sentence as well.

He rallied his resolution. The thing must not happen. Wasn't that his entire purpose? Why else would he be dressed like this?

Having reassured an anxious Brob, he went ashore in a dinghy rowed by two marines, and struck off inland. Night fell as he strode, but a moon and a half illuminated the dirt road for him. Apart from the warmth and scratchiness of his clothes, the uphill walk was no hardship; he was still young, and had always been athletic—formerly a champion in both track and basketball.

Loneliness did begin to oppress him. Save for farmsteads scattered over the landscape, the coziness of whose lamplit windows reminded him far too much of home, he walked among trees and through pastures. Shadows bulked, menacing. He almost wished he had brought a firearm. But no, that might be construed as a threat, and generate resistance to his arguments. Persuasion seemed his solitary hope.

In due course he entered a forest, but soon

he welcomed its darkness, when he stood looking down into a valley ablaze with campfires.
Campaigning or not, Hokas liked to keep late
hours. Tents, more or less in rows, lined the
riverbanks; he saw fieldpieces gleam, the bulks
of the "horses" that drew them, a large and flag-
topped pavilion which must house Napoleon;
he heard a murmur of movement down there,
and occasional snatches of song. While this
Grand Army did not compare with the original,
it must number thousands.

Having picked a route, Alex began the
stealthy part of his trip. His pulse was loud in
his ears, but his feet were silent. The stalking
and photographing of wild animals had long
been a sport he followed.

Eventually he passed a couple of pickets,
who were too busy comparing amorous notes
to observe him. His limited French gave him
the impression that Madeleine was quite a
female—unless she was a pure fiction, which
was not unlikely. Farther on, he belly-crawled
around fires where soldiers sat tossing dice or
singing ballads that all seemed to have the
refrain *"Rataplan! Rataplan!"* Lanes between
tents offered better concealment yet.

And thus he did, indeed, come to the outsize shelter at the heart of the encampment.
From its centerpole a flag fluttered in the
night wind, bearing a golden *N* within a
wreath. Moonlight sheened off the muskets
and bayonets of half a dozen sentries who
stood, in blue uniforms and high shakos, before the entrance. A brighter glow spilled from

inside, out of an opened windowflap at the rear. Alex decided to peek through it before he declared himself.

He did—and drew a gasp of amazement.

Luxuriously furnished, the pavilion held a table on which lay the remnants of a dinner (it seemed to have been an attempt at turning a native flying reptiloid into chicken Marengo) and several empty bottles. Perhaps this was the reason why a rather small and stout Hoka kept a hand thrust inside his epauletted coat. He stood at another table, covered with maps and notes, around which four spectacularly uniformed officers of his race were gathered. It was the alien squatting on top, next to the oil lamp, who shocked Alex.

Had he straightened on his grasshopper-like legs, that being would not have reached a Hoka chin. His two arms were long and skinny, his torso a mere lump which his black, silver-ornamented clothes did nothing to make impressive. Gray-skinned and hairless, his head was a caricature of a man's—batwing ears, beady eyes, needle-sharp teeth, and a nose ten centimeters long, that waggled as he spoke in a voice suggestive of fingernails scratching a blackboard.

He was employing English, the most wide-spread language on Toka as it was through-out the spaceways. Probably he knew less French than Alex did, whereas Napoleon and his staff would have had abundant contact

with humanity before they assumed their present identities.

"You must seize the moment, sire," he urged. "Audacity, always audacity! What have we done hitherto, we and the Spanish troops, but march and countermarch? Not a single shot fired in anger. Madness! We must seek them out, attack and destroy them, at once. Else we will have them at our backs when the English, that nation of shopkeepers, arrive in force."

The Hoka Napoleon gestured with his free hand. "But we don't want to hurt the Spaniards," he objected. "After all, they are supposed to become my loyal subjects, under my cousin. *Du sublime au ridicule il n'y a qu'un pas*, as my distinguished predecessor put it after the retreat from Moscow."

"Nonetheless," hissed the alien, "we must take decisive action or else undergo an even worse disaster than that same retreat. What is the use of your military genius, my Emperor, if you won't exercise it?" He turned to another Hoka, whose fur was red rather than golden. "Marshal Ney, you've talked enough about your wish to lead gallant cavalry charges. Do you never propose to get out there and *do* it?"

"*Oui, Monsieur* Snith," replied that one, "although I had, um-m, seen myself as an avenger, or better yet a defender, and the Spanish haven't done us any actual harm."

So, thought Alex, the alien's name was Snith. He had already recognized whence the being hailed. As he had suspected, this was a member of the Kratch. Now he knew, beyond doubt, that the Universal Nationalist Party which held power on their world had begun actively to undermine the wardship system and thus weaken the entire Interbeing League. Out of discord among the stars could come war; out of war, chaos; out of chaos, hegemony for those who had anticipated events.

"Hear me," the Krat was saying. "Has not my counsel put you on the way to power and glory? Do you not want to bring your species under a single rule, and so prepare it to deal equally with those that now dominate space? Then you must be prepared to follow my plans to the end." He lowered his voice. "Else, my Emperor, I fear that my government must terminate its altruistic efforts on your behalf, and I go home, leaving you to your fate."

The Hokas exchanged glances, somewhat daunted. Clearly, Snith had instigated their grandiosity, and continued to inspire and guide it. For his part, Alex felt sickened. Well, he thought, he'd wait till the conference was over and Snith had sought his quarters, then rouse Napoleon and set forth a quite different point of view—

A bayonet pricked his rump. "Yipe!" escaped from him. Turning, he confronted the sentries. They must have heard his heavy breathing and come to investigate.

"Qui va là?" demanded their corporal.

Alex mastered dismay. If the Hokas were reluctant to attack their fellow planetarians, they would be still more careful of a human. A face-to-face showdown with Snith might even change their minds. "Show some respect, *poilu!*" he rapped. "Don't you see who I am?"

"*Je ne suis pas—Monsieur*, I am not a *poilu*, I am an old *moustache*," said the corporal, offended. "And 'ere by my side is Karl Schmitt, a German grenadier lately returned from captivity in Russia—"

Alex's whirling thought was that these French could not have studied their Napoleonic history very closely either. The Emperor himself interrupted the discussion, by stumping over to the opening. "*Mon Dieu!*" he exclaimed. "*Mais c'est Monsieur le Plenipotentiaire* Jones! Sir, is this not irregular? The use of diplomatic channels is more in accord with the dignity of governments."

Snith reacted fast. "Ah, ha!" he shrilled. "There you see, my Emperor, how the Earthlings who have so long oppressed your world despise you. Avenge this insult to the honor of France!"

Alex reacted just as fast, although he was operating mainly on intuition. "Nonsense," he said. "In point of fact, I'm being—I mean I am none less than the Duke of Wellington, dispatched by none less than the Prince Regent, the Prime Minister, the First Lord of the Admiralty, Lord Nelson, and Commodore Hornblower, on a special mission to negotiate peace between our countries."

He drew himself up to his full height and did his best to fix Snith with a steely eye.

216

"Hein?" Napoleon gripped his stomach harder than before. "Now I am confused, me. Quick, a carafe of Courvoisier."

Snith jittered about on the table. "Where is your diplomatic accreditation, miserable Earthling?" he squealed, waving his tiny fists. "How will we be sure you are not a spy, or an assassin, or a—a—"

"A shopkeeper," suggested Marshal Ney.

"Thank you. A shopkeeper. My Emperor," said Snith more calmly, "a British ship must have brought him. Else he would have flown in like an honest plenipotentiary. Therefore he must be in collusion with perfidious Albion. Arrest him, sire, confine him, until we can discover what new threat lies in wait for you."

Under the gaze of his marshals, Napoleon could not but be strict. "Indeed," he said regretfully. *"Monsieur le Duc,* if such you are and if your intentions are sincere, you shall have a formal apology. Meanwhile, you will understand the necessity of detaining you. It shall be an honorable detention, whether or not we must afterward place you before a firing squad." To the soldiers: *"Enfermez-il, mes enfants."*

In a kind of dull consternation, Alex realized that his image required him to go off, a prisoner, too stoic to utter any protest.

First Napoleon took custody of his sword, and under Snith's waspish direction he was searched for hidden weapons, communications devices, and anything else of possible use. If only he had had a portable radio transceiver along, he could have called Brob at the instant things went awry. The giant could gently but firmly have freed him. Why didn't he think of simple precautions like that beforehand? A fine secret agent he was! The excuse that he wasn't supposed to be a secret agent, and moreover had had a good deal else on his mind, rang false.

The squad conducted him to a nearby farmhouse. They turned the family out, but those didn't object, since the Emperor had ordered they be well paid for the inconvenience. Alex had often thought that the Hokas were basically a sweeter species than humankind. Perhaps a theologian would suppose they were without original sin. The trouble was, they had too much originality of other sorts.

The house was humble, actually a cottage. A door at either end gave on a living room, which doubled as the dining room, a kitchen and scullery, and two bedrooms, all in a row along a narrow hall. The floor was clay, the furnishings few and mostly homemade. When the windows had been shuttered and barred on the outside, Alex's sole light would be from some candles in wooden holders.

"I give myself, me, ze honor to stand first watch outside ze south door," said the squad leader. "Corporal Sans-Souci, at Your Lordship's service. Karl, *mon brave*, I reward your *esprit* and command of English by posting you at ze north end."

"*Viel Danke, mein tapfere Korporal*," replied

the little German grenadier. "If *der Herzog* Vellington vould like to discuss de military sciences vit' me, please chust to open de door."

Jealousy made Sans-Souci bristle. *"Monsieur le Duc* is a man of ze most virile, *non?"* he countered. "If it should please 'im to describe 'is conquests in ze fields of love, and 'ear about mine, my door shall stand open too."

"No, thanks, to you both," Alex muttered, stumbled on into the cottage, and personally closed it up. He knew that, while either trooper would happily chatter for hours, exit would remain forbidden. Despite their size, Hokas were stronger than humans, and these must have a stubborn sense of duty.

Alex sank down onto a stool, put elbows on knees and face in hands. What a ghastly mess! Outnumbered as they were, the British could do nothing to rescue him. If they tried, they would be slaughtered, which was precisely what Snith wanted. Brob—No, Alex's idea about that being had been mistaken. Cannon and bullets meant nothing to Brob, but Snith undoubtedly had energy weapons against which not even the spacefarer could stand.

Could he, Alex, talk Napoleon into releasing him? Quite likely he could—for example, by an appeal to the Emperor's concern for the diplomatic niceties—except, again, for the ever-damned Snith. The Krat had the edge; he could outargue the man, whose position was, after all, a bit dubious in the eyes of the French (and in his own eyes, for that matter). Thus, if Alex was not actually shot, he would at least languish captive for weeks, probably after being moved to a secret locale. Meanwhile Snith would have egged Napoleon into an attack on the Spanish army, and shortly thereafter Nelson's assembled fleet would begin raiding the coasts and landing British troops, and before the League could do anything to prevent it, there would have been wholesale death and devastation. No doubt it would also occur elsewhere on Toka. Snith might be the leading Kratch agent, but obviously he had others doing the same kind of dirty work in chosen societies around the planet.

Wearily and drearily, Alex decided he might as well go to bed. In truth, that was his best course. Sometimes in the past, when he slept on a problem, his subconscious mind, uninhibited by the rationality of his waking self, had thrown up a solution crazy enough to work. The trouble now was, he doubted he could sleep.

He rose to his feet, and stopped cold. His glance had encountered an object hanging on the wall. It was a small leather bag, stoppered and bulging. This being a Spanish home, it must be a *bota*, and that word translated as "wineskin."

Alex snatched it to him, opened it and his mouth, and squeezed. A jet of raw, potent liquor laved his throat.

A deep buzz wakened him. Something brushed his nose. Blindly, aware mainly of a

220

headache and a raging thirst, he swatted. The something bumbled away. Its drone continued. Soon it was back. Alex unlidded a bleary eye. Light trickled in through cracks and warps in the shutters across his bedroom window. A creature the size of his thumb fluttered clumsily, ever closer to him. Multiple legs brushed his skin again. *"Damn,"* he mumbled, and once more made futile swatting motions.

The insectoid was as persistent as a Terrestrial fly. Maybe an odor of booze on his breath attracted it. Alex would get no more rest while it was loose.

He forced himself to alertness. Craftily, he waited. The huge brown bug hummed nearer. Alex remained motionless. His tormentor drew within centimeters of him. He kept himself quiet while he studied its flying pattern. Back and forth it went, on spatulate wings. Uzz, uzz, uzz it went. Alex mentally rehearsed his move. Then, pantherlike, his hand pounced. Fingers closed on the creature. "Gotcha!" he rasped. A sorry triumph, no doubt, but better than no triumph at all.

The bug fluttered in his grip. He was about to crush it, but stopped. Poor thing, it had meant him no harm. Why must he add even this bit to the sum of tragedy that would soon engulf Toka? (What a metaphor! But he was hung over, as well as oppressed by the doom he foresaw.) At the same time, he was jolly well not going to let it disturb his sleep any more.

He could carry it to a door, have that door

swung aside, and release his prisoner. But then the sentinel would be eager to talk to *his* prisoner, and that was just too much to face at this hour.

Alex swung his nude body out of bed. A chamber pot stood nearby. He raised the lid, thrust the bug inside, and dropped the lid back in place. The bug flew about. Resonance made the vessel boom hollowly. Alex realized he had not done the most intelligent thing possible, unless the house contained another chamber pot.

He looked around him. Daylight must be very new, at sunrise or before, since it was weak and gray. In a while someone would bring him breakfast. He hoped it would include plenty of strong black coffee. Afterward he would insist on a hot bath. Damnation, here he was, unwashed, uncombed, unshaven, confined in a peasant's hovel. Was that any way to treat the Duke of Wellington?

As abruptly as the night before, Alex froze. Now his gaze did not stop at a leather flask, which in any case lay flaccid and empty. Figuratively, his vision pierced the wall and soared over valley and hills to the sea. Inspiration had, indeed, come to him.

It might be sheer lunacy. The chances were that it was. He had no time for Hamlet-like hesitation. Nor did he have much to lose. Seizing the pot, he hurried out of the room and down the hall to the north end of the cottage. He had changed his mind about conversation with his guards.

*   *   *

None the worse for a sleepless night, Karl flung wide the door when Alex knocked, though his muscular little form continued to block any way out. Mist had drenched his uniform, and as yet blurred view of the camp below this farmstead, but reveilles had begun to sound through the chill air.

"*Gut Morgen, gut Morgen!*" the grenadier greeted. "Did de noble captiff shlumber vell? Mine duty ends soon, but I vill be glad to shtay and enchoy discourse *am Krieg*—"

He broke off, surprised. M-m-uzzz, oom, oom went the jar that Alex held in the crook of an arm.

"Mine lord," Karl said after a moment, in a tone of awe, "you iss a powerful man, t'rough and t'rough. I vill be honored to empty dot for you."

"No need." Alex took the lid off and tilted the vessel forward. The bug blundered forth. As it rose higher, sunrise light from behind the fog made it gleam like metal. Karl's astounded stare followed it till it was out of sight.

Thereafter he scratched his head with his bayonet and murmured, "I haff heard dey feed dem terrible on de English ships, but *vot vas dot?*"

Alex smiled smugly, laid a finger alongside his nose, and replied in a mysterious voice, "I'm afraid I can't tell you that, old chap. Military secrets, don't y' know."

Karl's eyes grew round. *"Mein Herr?* Zecrets? But ve gafe you a zearch last night."

"Ah, well, we humans—for I am human, you realize, as well as being the Duke of Wellington —we have our little tricks," Alex answered. He assumed a confidential manner. "You're familiar with the idea of carrier pigeons. Before you became a German grenadier, you may have heard about our Terrestrial technology— miniaturization, transistors—but I may say no more. Except this, because you're stout and true, Karl, whether or not you're on the wrong side in this war. No matter what happens later today, never blame yourself. You could not possibly have known."

He closed the door on the shaken Hoka, set the mug aside, and sought the south end of the house.

"Bonjour, monsieur," hailed Sans-Souci. "I 'ope ze noble lord 'as slept well?"

"Frankly, no," said Alex. "I'm sure you can guess why."

The soldier cocked his ears beneath his shako. *"Eh, bien,* ze gentleman, 'e 'as been lonely, *n'est-ce pas?"*

Alex winked, leered, and dug a thumb into the other's ribs. "We're men of the world, you and I, corporal. The difference in our stations makes no difference. . . . Uh, I mean a man's a man's for a' that, and—Anyhow, if I'm to be detained, don't you agree I should have . . . companionship?"

Sans-Souci grew ill at ease. " 'Ow true, 'ow

sad. But Your Lordship, 'e is not of our species—"

Alex drew himself up to his full height. "What do you think I am?" he snapped. "I have nothing in mind but a lady of my race."

"Zat will not be so easy, I fear."

"Perhaps easier than you think, corporal. This is what I want you to do for me. When you're relieved, pass the word on to your lieutenant that, if the Emperor is virile enough to understand, which he undoubtedly is, why, then the Emperor will order a search for a nice, strapping wench. There are a number of humans on Toka, you recall—League personnel, scientists, journalists, lately even an occasional tourist. I happen to know that some are right in this area. It should not be difficult to contact them and—Well, corporal, if this works out, you'll find me not ungrateful."

Sans-Souci slapped his breast. "Ah, *monsieur*," he cried, "to 'elp love blossom, zat will be its own reward!"

A couple of new soldiers appeared out of the fog and announced that they were the next guards. Sans-Souci barely took time to introduce them to the distinguished detainee— a stolid, though hard-drinking private from Normandy and a dashing Gascon sergeant of Zouaves—before hastening off. Alex heard a clatter from behind the house as Karl departed equally fast.

Returning inside, the man busied himself in preparations for that which he hoped would transpire. Whatever did, he should not have long to wait. Any collection of Hokas was an incredible rumor mill. What the sentries had to relate should be known to the whole Grand Army within the hour.

Excitement coursed through his blood and drove the pain out of his head. Win, lose, or draw, by gosh and by golly, he was back in action!

He estimated that a mere thirty minutes had passed when the door to the main room opened again, from outside. At first he assumed a trooper was bringing his breakfast, then he remembered that English aristocrats slept notoriously late and Napoleon would not want his guest disturbed without need. Then a being stepped through, closed the door behind him, and glared.

It was Snith.

"What's this?" the Krat screamed. The volume of the sound was slight, out of his minuscule lungs.

"What's what?" asked Alex, careful to move slowly. Though he towered a full meter above the alien, and probably outmassed him tenfold, Snith carried a dart gun at his belt; and his race was more excitable, impatient, irascible than most.

"You know what's what, you wretch. That communication device of yours, and that camp of your abominable co-humans somewhere close by. Thought you'd sneak one over on me, did you? Ha! I'm sharper than you guessed, Jones. Already scouts have brought back word of those English in the bay and the village. We'll move on them this very day. But first I want to know what else to expect, Jones, and you'll tell me. Immediately!"

"Let's be reasonable," Alex temporized. While he had expected Snith to arrive alone, lest the Hokas learn too much, he could not predict the exact course of events—merely devise a set of contingency plans. "Don't you realize what harm you're doing on this planet? Not only to it, either. If ever word gets out about your government's part in this, you can be sure the rest of the League will move to have it replaced."

The Krat sneered upward at the human's naked height. "They won't know till far too late, those milksop pacifists. By then, Universal Nationalism will dominate a coalition so powerful that—Stand back, you! Not a centimeter closer, or I shoot." He touched the gun in its holster.

"What use would that be to you?" Alex argued. "Dead men tell no tales."

"Ah, but you wouldn't be dead, Jones. The venom in these darts doesn't kill unless they strike near the heart. In a leg, say, they'll make you feel as though you're burning alive. Oh, you'll talk, you'll talk," responded Snith, obviously enjoying his own ruthlessness. "Why not save yourself the agony? But you'd better tell the truth, or else, afterward, you'll wish you had. How you'll wish you had!"

"Well, uh, well—Look, excuse me, I have to

take a moment for nature. How can I concentrate unless I do?"

"Hurry up, then," Snith ordered.

Alex went to the chamber pot. He bent down as if to remove its lid. Both his hands closed on its body. Faster than when he had captured the bug, he hurled it. As a youth in the Naval Academy, he had been a basketball star. The old reflexes were still there. The lid fell free as the mug soared. Upside down, it descended on Snith. Too astonished to have moved, the Krat buckled beneath that impact. Alex made a flying tackle, landed on the pot and held it secure.

Snith banged on it from within, boomlay, boomlay, boomlay, boom. "What's the meaning of this outrage?" came his muffled shriek. "Let me go, you fiend!"

"Heh, heh, heh," taunted Alex. He dragged the container over the floor to a chair whereon lay strips of cloth torn off garments left by the dwellers here. Reaching beneath, he hauled Snith out. Before the Krat could draw weapon, he was helpless in the grasp of a far stronger being. Alex disarmed him, folded him with knees below jaws, and began tying him.

"Help, murder, treason!" Snith cried. As expected, his thin tones did not penetrate the door.

He regained a measure of self-control. "You're mad, insane," he gabbled. "How do you imagine you can escape? What will Napoleon do if you've harmed his . . . his Talleyrand? Stop this, Jones, and we can reach some *modus vivendi*."

"Yeah, sure," grunted Alex. He gagged his captive and left him trussed on the floor.

Heart pounding, the man spread out the disguise he had improvised from raiment and bedding. Thus far his plan had succeeded better than he dared hope, but now it would depend on his years of practice at playing out roles before Hokas, for the costume would never have gotten by a human.

First he donned his Wellingtonian greatcoat. Into a capacious pocket he stuffed the weakly struggling Snith. Thereafter he wrapped his hips in a blanket, which simulated a skirt long enough to hide the boots he donned, and his upper body in a dress which had belonged to the housewife and which on him became a sort of blouse. Over all he pinned another blanket, to be a cloak with a cowl, and from that hood he hung a cheesecloth veil.

Here goes nothing, he thought, and minced daintily, for practice, through the cottage to the farther door. It opened at his knock. An astonished Sergeant Le Galant gaped at the spectacle which confronted him. He hefted his musket. "*Qui va là?*" he demanded in a slightly stunned voice.

Alex waved a languid hand. "Oh, sir," he answered falsetto, "please let me by. I'm so tired. His Grace the Duke is a . . . a most vigorous gentleman. Oh, dear, and to think I forgot to bring my smelling salts."

The Hoka's suspicions dissolved in a burst of

romanticism. Naturally, he took for granted that the lady had entered from the side opposite. *"Ah, ma belle petite,"* he burbled, while he kissed Alex's hand, "zis is a service you 'ave done not only for *Monsieur le Duc*, but for France. We 'ave our reputation to maintain, *non? Mille remerciments. Adieu, et au revoir."*

Sighing, he watched Alex sway off.

The mists had lifted, and everywhere Hoka soldiers stared at the strange figure, whispered, nudged each other, and nodded knowingly. A number of them blew kisses. Beneath his finery, Alex sweated. He must not move fast, or they would start to wonder; yet he must get clear soon, before word reached Napoleon and made *him* wonder.

His freedom was less important than the prisoner he carried, and had been set at double hazard for that exact reason. This, maybe, was the salvation of Toka. Maybe.

When he had climbed the ridge and entered the forest, Alex shouted for joy. Henceforward he, as a woodsman, would undertake to elude any pursuit. He cast the female garb from him. Attired in greatcoat and boots, the pleni-potentiary of the Interbeing League marched onward to the sea.

At his insistence, the flotilla recalled its marines and sought open water before the French arrived. Nelson grumbled that retreat was not British, but the human mollified him by describing the move as a strategic withdrawal for purposes of consolidation.

In Alex's cabin, he and Brob confronted Snith. The diminutive Krat did not lack courage. He crouched on the bunk and spat defiance. "Never will I betray the cause! Do your worst! And afterward, try to explain away my mangled body to your lily-livered superiors."

"Torture is, needless to say, unthinkable," Brob agreed. "Nevertheless, we must obtain the information that will enable us to thwart your plot against the peace. Would you consider a large bribe?"

Alex fingered his newly smooth chin and scowled. The ship heeled to the wind. Sunlight scythed through ports to glow on panels. He heard waves rumble and whoosh, timbers creak, a cheerful sound of music and dance from the deck; he caught a whiff of fresh salt air; not far off, if he flew, were Tanni and the kids. . . . Yes, he thought, this was a lovely world in a splendid universe, and must be kept that way.

"Bribe?" Snith was retorting indignantly. "The bribe does not exist which can buy a true Universal Nationalist. No, you are doomed, you decadent libertarians. You may have kidnapped me, but elsewhere the sacred cause progresses apace. Soon the rest of this planet will explode, and blow you onto the ash heap of history."

Alex nodded to himself. A nap had done wonders for him akin to those which had happened ashore. Pieces of the puzzle clicked together, almost audibly.

Conspirators were active in unknown places around the globe. They must be rather few, though; Snith appeared to have managed the entire Napoleonic phase by himself. They must, also, have some means of communication, a code; and they must be ready at any time to meet for consultation, in case of emergency. Yes. The basic problem was how to summon them. Snith knew the code and the recognition signals, but Snith wasn't telling. However, if you took into account the feverish Kratch temperament—

A slow grin spread across Alex's face. "Brob," he murmured, "we have an extra stateroom for our guest. But he should not be left to pine in isolation, should he? That would be cruel. I think I can get the captain to release you from your duties as mate, in order that you can stay full time with Mr. Snith."

"What for?" asked the spacefarer, surprised.

Alex rubbed his hands together. "Oh, to try persuasion," he said. "You're a good, kind soul, Brob. If anybody can convince Mr. Snith of the error of his ways, it's you. Keep him company. Talk to him. You might, for instance, tell him about flower arrangements."

The planet had barely rotated through another of its 24.35-hour days when Snith, trembling and blubbering, yielded.

It was necessary to choose the rendezvous with care. The conspirators weren't stupid. Upon receiving their enciphered messages, which bore Snith's name and declared that unforeseen circumstances required an immediate conference, they would look at their maps. They would check records of whatever intelligence they had concerning human movements and capabilities at the designated spot. If anything appeared suspicious, they would stay away. Even if nothing did, they would fly in with such instruments as metal detectors wide open, alert for any indications of a trap.

Accordingly, Alex had made primitive arrangements. After picking up a long-range transmitter in Plymouth, he directed *Victory*—alone—to an isolated Cornish cove, whence he issued his call. Inland lay nothing but a few small, widely scattered farms. Interstellar agents would think naught of a single windjammer anchored offshore, nor imagine that marines and bluejackets lurked around the field where they were supposed to land—when those Hokas were armed simply with truncheons and belaying pins.

Night fell. All three moons were aloft. Frost rings surrounded them. Trees hemmed in an expanse of several hectares, whereon haystacks rested hoar; the nearest dwelling was kilometers off. Silence prevailed, save when wildfowl hooted. Alex shivered where he crouched in the woods. Twigs prickled him. He wanted a drink.

Ashimmer beneath moons and stars, a teardrop shape descended, the first of the enemy vehicles. It grounded on a whisper of forcefield, but did not open at once. Whoever was inside must be satisfying himself that nothing of menace was here.

A haystack scuttled forward. It had been glued around Brob. Before anybody in the car could have reacted, he was there. His right fist smashed through its fuselage to the radio equipment. His left hand peeled back the metal around the engine and put that out of commission.

"At 'em, boys!" Alex yelled. His followers swarmed forth to make the arrest. They were scarcely necessary. Brob had been quick to disarm and secure the two beings within.

Afterward he tucked the car out of sight under a tree and returned to being a haystack, while Alex and the Hokas concealed themselves again.

In this wise, during the course of the night, they collected thirty prisoners, the entire ring. Its members were not all Kratch. Among them were two Slissii, a Pornian, a Sarennian, a Worbenite, three Chakbans; but the Kratch were preponderant, and had clearly been the leaders.

A glorious victory! Alex thought about the administrative details ahead of him, and moaned aloud.

Two weeks later, though, at home, rested and refreshed, he confronted Napoleon. The Empire was his most pressing problem. Mongols, Aztecs, Crusaders, and other troublesome types were rapidly reverting to an approximation of normal, now that the sources of their inspiration had been exposed and discredited. But Imperial France not only had a firmer base, it had the unrelenting hostility of Georgian Britain. The Peace of Amiens, which Alex had patched together, was fragile indeed.

Tanni was a gracious hostess and a marvelous cook. The plenipotentiary's household staff, and his children, were on their best behavior. Candlelight, polished silver, snowy linen, soft music had their mellowing effect. At the same time, the awesome presence of Brob reminded the Emperor—who was, after all, sane in his Hoka fashion—that other worlds were concerned about this one. The trick was to provide him and his followers an alternative to the excitement they had been enjoying.

"Messire," Alex urged over the cognac and cigars, "as a man of vision, you surely realize with especial clarity that the future is different from the past. You yourself, a mover and shaker, have shown us that the old ways can never be the same again, but instead we must move on to new things, new opportunities—*la carrière ouverte aux talents*, as your illustrious namesake phrased it. If you will pardon my accent."

Napoleon shifted in his chair and clutched his stomach. "Yes, *mais oui*, I realize this in principle," he answered unhappily. "I have some knowledge of history, myself. Forty centuries look down upon us. But you must realize in your turn, *Monsieur le Plenipotentiaire*, that a vast outpouring of energy has been released in France. The people will not return to their placid lives under the *ancien régime*. They have tasted adventure. They will always desire it."

Alex wagged his forefinger. Tanni's glance reminded him that this might not be the perfect gesture to make at the Emperor, and he hastily took up his drink. "Ah, but messire," he said, "think further, I beg you. You ask what will engage the interest of your populace, should the Grand Army be disbanded. Why, what else but the natural successor to the Empire? The Republic!"

"Qu'est-ce que vous dites?" asked Napoleon, and pricked up his ears.

"I comprehend, messire," Alex said. "Cares of state have kept you from studying what happened to Terrestrial France beyond your own period. Well, I have a number of books which I will gladly copy off for your perusal. I am sure you will find that French party politics can be more intricate and engaging than the most far-ranging military campaign." He paused. "In fact, messire, if you should choose to abdicate and stand for elective office, you would find the challenge greater than any you might have encountered at Austerlitz. Should you win your election, you will find matters more complicated than ever at Berezina or Waterloo. But go forward, indomitable, *mon petit caporal!*" he cried. *"Toujours l'audace!"*

Napoleon leaned over the table, breathing heavily. Moisture glistened on his black nose. Alex saw that he had him hooked.

* * *

At Mixumaxu spaceport, the Joneses bade Brob an affectionate farewell. "Do come back and see us," Tanni invited. "You're an old darling, did anybody ever tell you?" When he stooped to hug her, she kissed him full on his slightly radioactive mouth.

The couple returned to their residence in a less pleasant mood. Leopold Ormen had appeared at the city and applied for clearance to depart in his private spaceship.

Tanni begged to be excused from meeting him again. She felt too embarrassed. Alex insisted that she had made no mistake which he would not have made himself under the circumstances, but she refused anyway. Instead, she proposed, let her spend the time preparing a sumptuous dinner for the family; and then, after the children had gone to bed—

Thus Alex sat alone behind his desk when the journalist entered at the appointed hour. Ormen seemed to have lost none of his cockiness. "Well, Jones," he said, as he lowered himself into a chair and lit a cigarette, "why do I have to see you before I leave?"

"We've stuff to discuss," Alex answered, "like your involvement in the Kratch conspiracy."

Ormen gestured airily. "What are you talking about?" he laughed. "Me? I'm nothing but a reporter—and if perchance you get paranoid about me, that's a fact which I'll report.'

"Oh, I have no proof," Alex admitted. "The League investigation and the trials of the obviously guilty will drag on for years, I suppose. Meanwhile you'll come under the statute of limitations, damn it. But just between us, you were part and parcel of the thing, weren't you? Your job was to prepare the way for the Kratch, and afterward it would've been to write and televise the stories which would have brought our whole system down."

Ormen narrowed his eyes. "Those are pretty serious charges, Jones," he lipped thinly. "I wouldn't like your noising them around, even in private conversation. They could hurt me; and I don't sit still for being hurt. No, sir."

He straightened. "All right," he said, "let's be frank. You've found indications, not legal proof but indications, that would cause many of my audience and my readers to stop trusting me. But on my side—Jones, I've seen plenty on this planet. Maybe somehow you did pull your chestnuts out of the fire. But the incredible, left-handed way that you did it—not to mention the data I've gotten on your crazy, half-legal improvisations in the past—Let me warn you, Jones. If you don't keep quiet about me, I'll publish stories that will destroy you."

From his scalp to his toes, a great, tingling warmth rushed through Alex. He had nothing to fear. True, in the course of his duties he had often fallen into ridiculous positions, but this had taught him indifference to ridicule. As for his record of accomplishment, it spoke for itself. Nobody could have bettered it. Nobody in his right mind would want to try. Until such time as he had brought them to full autonomy, Alexander Jones was the indispensable man among the Hokas.

He could not resist. Rising behind the desk, he drew himself to his full height, fixed Leopold Ormen with a steely eye, and rapped out: *"Publish and be damned!"*

Publisher's Note: It has been noted elsewhere that some ideas are so dumb that only intellectuals can believe them. Particularly, left-wing intellectuals. We offer the following as proof.

AFTERWORD

"The Bear That Walks Like a Man":
An Ursinoid Stereotype in Early Interbeing
Era Popular Culture
by
S*ndr* M**s*l[1]

A brief critique of the notorious Hoka stories by P. Anderson and G. R. Dickson offers one of the simplest, yet surest, means of exposing the speciesist sham that was the prerevolutionary Interbeing League. Now that we have cast off those ancient shackles of liberationist enslave-

---

[1] Academician of the All-Systems Institute for Historico-Literary Investigations

ment and discarded our bourgeois blindfolds, we can finally attain ideologically correct insights into the justly anathematized follies of past centuries.

Let none be misled by the seemingly innocuous content or the trivial import of the historical fiction under examination here. Innocence is an untenable posture for species chauvinists. When the ironic whimsies of Anderson and Dickson are compared with the stark reality of blaster-waving humans tyrannizing the peace-loving Hokas, their purported humor stands revealed as a cunning cloak— even a coarse rationalization—for human imperialist aspirations.

Although some decadent twentieth century neo-colonialists perceived "popular culture" as an unerring index of a society's actual (as opposed to feigned) values, in the hands of scholars wholly dedicated to working-class interests, such analysis has become a matchless weapon in the ongoing revolutionary struggle. A close reading of the Hoka stories unmasks as blatant lies the reactionaries' prattle about "freedom," "development," and "universal siblinghood" disseminated via the human-biased charter of the Interbeing League. An admission that this ostensibly neutral organization was but a thinly disguised front for Earth's hegemonistic ambitions is found in a surviving memorandum of a highly placed human official: ". . . of all fully civilized races, it is humankind, the predominant species whose culture sets the tone of the entire

League, that most feels the impact of *noblesse oblige.*"

The very name of the first Hoka collection, *Earthman's Burden,* is fraught with ominous connotations inasmuch as it is a crude word-play on an infamous phrase by R. Kipling, whom the text styles "a great poet whose prescient spirit animates our entire endeavor." Writers who draw inspiration from doggerel penned by a jingoistic journalist must arouse immediate suspicions in every right-minded critic. Lest anyone claim that the League did in fact magnanimously "work another's gain" on the planet Toka, recent studies by Tyrell, *et al.* conclusively demonstrate the contrary. When due weight is accorded social as well as monetary factors, the profits reaped by off-worlders far exceeded League expenditures on the Hokas. (For example, while media royalties for Hoka characters fattened the purses of Earthbound plutocrats, the League mission on Toka remained scandalously understaffed—not a single welfare functionary was accredited there during the entire League era.)

League-Hoka relations were tainted from the very moment of Toka's discovery by P. G. Brackney, a veritable Stamford Raffles of the spaceways. This infamous individualist, whose name formerly bespattered one entire spiral arm of our galaxy, called the Tokan sun "Brackney's Star" after his own egomaniac self. Efforts to persuade the autochthones to replace this odious designation with a more socially responsible one such as "Rigor,"

"Communard," or "Unity," have not yet met with success. (See the appropriate report of the Central Committee for the Adjustment of Pre-Revolutionary Nomenclature.)

Despite an avowed policy of non-intervention, cryptocolonialist meddling by the first League survey team irreparably altered conditions on Toka. Precipitous introduction of industrialism elevated the technophilic urban elites of Mixumaxu and other embryonic polities (the so-called "Five-and-a-Half-Cities") at the expense of the hinterland's agrarian masses. While the latter were being exploited to feed their bloated oppressors via stockraising, they were being simultaneously indoctrinated with the appalling myths of the American Old West that beguiled them into imagining their bondage to be perfect liberty.

Not only did this intrusive infusion of human culture realign class relationships among the Hokas, it also upset the ancient equilibrium between the ursinoid Hokas and the reptilian Slissii. Had political development proceeded at its natural pace, a bispeciesist communal society would have inevitably evolved on Toka. Alas, the shameful promammalianist prejudices of the human interlopers tipped the scales towards the furred moiety of the indigenous population. Although the remark traditionally attributed to the first Survey captain—*"Timeo dracones et dona ferentis"*—may well be apocryphal, it expresses his species' well-documented aversion to the "dragon-like" Slissii. Surely it is no accident that the next starship dispatched to Toka was the *H.M.S. Draco*.

Once infected by the imperialism of the bigoted tutors they sought to ape, the Hokas usurped Slissii territory. The reptiloids' valiant struggle to recover their lost ancestral homelands would have ultimately achieved its worthy goal but for the untimely intervention of the insidious Alexander Braithwaite Jones which is related in "The Sheriff of Canyon Gulch." (Incontrovertible evidence of the conspiracy and deliberately staged "accident" that placed him on the planetary scene have but recently come to light. See the brilliant reconstruction of events by Tief-Gurgel.)

Although in their contemptible bourgeois fashion Anderson and Dickson attempt to portray Jones as a bumbling simpleton of a hero, it is well known that he was in actuality a cunning arch-villain steeped in reactionary paternalism of the deepest hue. This lackey of the League's ruling caste soon entangled the all-too-trusting Hokas in that vilest of crimes— genocide. Obviously, unconfessed racial guilt for complicity in the extirpation of the Slissii people is a prime factor influencing subsequent Hoka-human relations. Jones' own memoranda recount the Hokas' morbid remorse, their half-hearted fumbles at compensation for the pitiful survivors of the massacres, and their feeble rationalizations about the Slissii prospering in exile—as if mere monetary recompense could ever erase the reptiloids' memories of suffering.

Indeed, the obsessively imitative behavior of the Hokas toward humans is a servile response typical of oppressed peoples. They emulate their vile oppressors in the deluded hope of thereby bettering their own conditon. Such doomed ambitions were encouraged by Jones' lying promises of accelerated advancement in planetary legal status. Although he led his first delegation of Hokas to Earth shortly after his appointment as plenipotenary (the chaotic expedition is described in "Don Jones"), promotion to full League membership had still not occurred decades later at the time of his last fictionalized adventure, "The Napoleon Crime."

The intervening years were filled with disedifying incidents. "In Hoka Signo Vinces" purports to tell how the Hokas took the deplorable aggressiveness inspired by human models into space with an unprovoked attack on a Pornian peacekeeping dreadnaught. The assault is suspiciously similar to the *Clampherdown* affair lauded by the cryptofeudalist Kipling. The drug smuggling that holds center stage in "The Adventure of the Misplaced Hound" merely demonstrates the pervasive moral depravity of the League. "Yo Ho Hoka" shows the ursinoids engaging in piracy, an occupation unknown among them until copied from humans. Such intraspecies conflict strikes an ominous new note in Hoka history, foreshadowing the strife that erupts in "The Napoleon Crime." And if random outbursts of violence were not sufficiently reprehensible, the Hokas fell so low as to institutionalize their newly stimulated appetite for aggression and to glorify militarism in "The Tiddlywink Warriors." "Joy in Mudville" records the perversion and circumvention of the socially beneficial purposes of healthful sport for the contemptible glamorization of individual players and species. "Undiplomatic Immunity" boasts of the collaboration by Hoka pawns in human-engineered espionage schemes—as if this were an occasion for praise and not blame. Even during Jones' absence from Toka his wife and son proved themselves scarcely less able participants in the galaxy-spanning imperialistic designs of the League, as recounted in "Full Pack (Hokas Wild)."

While repressed genocidal guilt explains Hoka subservience, human dominance is surely an expression of barely concealed envy and fear of their sturdier siblings-in-fur. And if this motivation were not sufficiently obvious to the socially sensitized observer, Jones' own private disclosure of apprehension that the Hokas "may one day succeed us as the political leaders of the galaxy" places the matter beyond doubt.

A consistent pattern of self-aggrandizment coupled with condescending paternalism towards his "wards" runs through Jones' career. He automatically concludes on first meeting Hokas that "to them the humans were almost gods." (The terms "godling" and "demi-god" also loom scandalously large in his vocabulary.) He professes to feel like "an elder brother" towards the Hokas and describes them as "somewhat like small human children," while professing to "care for the little fellows as if they were my own."

The constant—nay, obsessive—emphasis on the Hokas' fortuitous resemblance to those outmoded human toys known as teddybears is more than just another manifestation of typical bourgeois sentimentality. It is insidious propaganda that represents a deliberate attempt to mold the very image of the Hoka species into a distorted shape more congenial to human purposes, to condition them to accept the degrading role of playthings that their overlords had chosen for them. The potential utility of the powerful ursinoid physique for meaningful labor is barely suggested.

And a more ominous reason than sheer political expedience underlies human reluctance to accord Hokas adult status: restricting them to a childish context keeps them safely neuter. (Recall that teddybears traditionally lack genitalia.) Note the implicit erotic content in a lubricious human female's response to Hokas: "They're just pure cuteness, with their adorable button noses and little round tummies." Doubtless the quadrimammary bodies of female Hokas drove the breast fetishists among contemporary human males to transports of gross ecstacy. (More than a suspicion of this attitude clings to Jones himself. See the acclaimed psychobiography by Black.) Likewise, the oft-reiterated datum about Hokas' prodigious capacity for alcohol should be read as a code for awesome capacity of quite another sort. And, of course, fur often seems sensuous to the furless.

Throughout history masters have always resented the sexuality of their slaves, imputing to it an animal vigor that both fascinates and repels. When, as on Toka, the oppressed class actually reminds the oppressors of brute animals and, moreover, willingly portrays alien beasts, xeno-sexual hostility can sink to unprecedented depths of depravity. (Was Jones soured by speculations as to the games his wife—perhaps perversely abetted by their son—might have played with the Hoka "Wolf Pack"? This compromising situation can be fully explained only when the unexpurgated critical edition of Tanni Jones' diary is finally published. Until then, the Hokas' choice of *Jungle Book* wolves to impersonate must stand as a significant, if unsubtle, symbol.)

Although the cleansing fire of revolutionary zeal has happily rendered such aberrations obsolete, speciesism in all its loathesomeness did pervade human behavior in the League era. See the disreputable pattern established on Hoka repeated elsewhere when Tanni Jones plays goddess for the Telks or when her husband lusts after the comely Bagdadburghess. Note the overwhelmingly bigoted characterizations of non-Hoka alien peoples in these stories. Observe the sly malice of the authors in transcribing honorable off-Earth names so as to suggest derogatory puns (e.g.: Pornians, ppussjans, Porkelans, Kratch). But for the disturbing presence of manipulative humans, Hokas could not possibly have become embroiled in these interspecies conflicts, since as is well known, at a sufficiently high level of cultural and political development, all peoples will inevitably and invariably evolve peaceloving collectivist societies.

Geraldo and others have proposed that humans were covertly grooming the Hokas to become their galactic janissaries once the "democratic" sham of the League could be replaced by an overtly expansionist human Empire. This shocking hypothesis has much to commend it, for the selection of literary models to which the hapless ursinoids were exposed can scarcely be as accidental as depicted. Would pure chance alone have brought to the Hokas' attention such offscourings of nineteenth and twentieth century imperialism as R. Kipling, A. C. Doyle, R. L. Stevenson, P. C. Wren, E. L. Thayer, E. P. Oppenheim, C. S. Forrester, and—too shuddersome to specify—American mass media? Performing Mozart's *Don Juan* before the Hoka delegation is likewise suspect, given the licentious, superstitious, and pro-aristocratic nature of this opera. Ever the opportunists, devious human corrupters could turn any circumstance to their advantage.

A brief survey cannot begin to enumerate each of the League's vile crimes against Toka. (For an exhaustive treatment, see fascicle #1848 by Redstone and Clootie in *Annalen des Imperialismus*.) The insidious and ubiquitous employment of bourgeois human cultural products as vectors of contagion merits unreserved condemnation by all progressive peoples. But the blatant hypocrisy of the oppressors, their unconvincing invocation of random chance or individual actions as causative factors rather than the inexorable pressure of trans-historical forces, must ignite our righteous indignation to nova-bright fury. The tragic experience of the Hokas still stands as a unique incitement to ceaseless and vigilant revolutionary struggle.

In this respect Anderson and Dickson have unwittingly fostered the liberationist cause. Their fictionalized chronicles of Toka make such excellent supplementary reading for introductory political philosophy courses; this justifies reproducing material otherwise worthy of immediate suppression. Allegations that some hooliganistic students find the stories humorous should not be allowed to call their educational utility into question.

The issue of the authors' personal culpability as League propagandists merits consideration. They are reputed to have felt a certain empathy towards the ursinoids, although witnesses differ as to which partner more resembled a Hoka and, indeed, exactly what form this supposed similarity took. Nevertheless, Anderson and Dickson docilely adhered to the League's speciesist line in the Hoka stories.

However, at the risk of urging an unseemly bourgeois magnanimity, we cautiously suggest that these writers be placed in the context of their own times, as dupes of the then-dominant ruling clique rather than as deliberate enemies of the people. Their experiments in social criticism lie outside the Hoka canon but do exist. That Anderson's "Critique of Impure Reason" so brilliantly dissects the very type of decadent contemporary literature admired by would-be poet Jones and that Dickson's "Zeepsday" deftly flays what passed for a legal system in those days, cannot fail to arouse regret that these writers did not have the opportunity of placing their undeniable talents wholly at the service of the working class.

And what of today's Hokas? Jones—for once—spoke rightly when he observed that "a Hoka is *not* a miniature human being" (italics his). It should be readily apparent by now, even to the oppression-warped ursinoids themselves, that they need humans as much as molluscs need motorbikes, which is to say, not at all. Alas, those generations of artful conditioning in retrograde thought have left the Hokas singularly unresponsive to the beauties of dialectical argument. Our most energetic and altruistic efforts to radicalize them have yielded nothing but frustration to date. (Misapplying ancient folk wisdom, some faint hearts have likened the enterprise to "taking a bear by the tooth.")

Drastic re-education has been tried and found sadly wanting. Although scholars using scanty records have painstakingly reconstructed the languages and cultures extant when the Hokas were in a state of nature, attempts to instruct the ursinoids in their ancestral ways have yet to raise them to revolutionary consciousness. (The Hokas reportedly play at being linguists and anthropologists instead.) Debate currently rages as to whether showing them the films of S. Eisenstein is a feasible alternative. However, apprehension about the possible impact of *Ivan the Terrible* on unprepared Hoka audiences has temporarily postponed implementation of this promsing approach. (The issue has been admirably summarized by Verkauf.)

Nevertheless, the tide of ideological progress rolls irresistably onward. Ultimate victory is certain. Surely the worthy ursinoids will soon be healed of the last vestiges of League influence. We eagerly await that glorious day when fully liberated Hokas assume their rightful place in the classless Union of Beings even now being forged in our own Sector and that will soon and inevitably liberate our entire Galaxy from the capitalist oppressors.

POUL ANDERSON
Winner of 7 Hugos and 3 Nebulas

☐	53088-8	CONFLICT	$2.95
	53089-6		Canada $3.50
☐	48527-1	COLD VICTORY	$2.75
☐	48517-4	EXPLORATIONS,	$2.50
☐	48515-8	FANTASY	$2.50
☐	48550-6	THE GODS LAUGHED	$2.95
☐	48579-4	GUARDIANS OF TIME	$2.95
☐	53567-7	HOKA! (with Gordon R. Dickson)	$2.75
	53568-5		Canada $3.25
☐	48582-4	LONG NIGHT	$2.95
☐	53079-9	A MIDSUMMER TEMPEST	$2.95
	53080-2		Canada $3.50
☐	48553-0	NEW AMERICA	$2.95
☐	48596-4	PSYCHOTECHNIC LEAGUE	$2.95
☐	48533-6	STARSHIP	$2.75
☐	53073-X	TALES OF THE FLYING MOUNTAINS	$2.95
	53074-8		Canada $3.50
☐	53076-4	TIME PATROLMAN	$2.95
	53077-2		Canada $3.50
☐	48561-1	TWILIGHT WORLD	$2.75
☐	53085-3	THE UNICORN TRADE	$2.95
	53086-1		Canada $3.50
☐	53081-0	PAST TIMES	$2.95
	53082-9		Canada $3.50

Buy them at your local bookstore or use this handy coupon:
Clip and mail this page with your order

TOR BOOKS—Reader Service Dept.
P.O. Box 690, Rockville Centre, N.Y. 11571

Please send me the book(s) I have checked above. I am enclosing
$_____ (please add $1.00 to cover postage and handling).
Send check or money order only—no cash or C.O.D.'s.

Mr./Mrs./Miss _____

Address _____

City _____ State/Zip _____

Please allow six weeks for delivery. Prices subject to change without
notice.

GORDON R. DICKSON

☐	53068-3	Hoka! (with Poul Anderson)	$2.95
	53069-1		Canada $3.50
☐	53556-1	Sleepwalkers' World	$2.95
	53557-X		Canada $3.50
☐	53564-2	The Outposter	$2.95
	53565-0		Canada $3.50
☐	48525-5	Planet Run	$2.75
		with Keith Laumer	
☐	48556-5	The Pritcher Mass	$2.75
☐	48576-X	The Man From Earth	$2.95
☐	53562-6	The Last Master	$2.95
	53563-4		Canada $3.50
☐	53550-2	BEYOND THE DAR AL-HARB	$2.95
	53551-0		Canada $3.50
☐	53558-8	SPACE WINNERS	$2.95
	53559-6		Canada $3.50
☐	53552-9	STEEL BROTHER	$2.95
	53553-7		Canada $3.50

Buy them at your local bookstore or use this handy coupon:
Clip and mail this page with your order

TOR BOOKS—Reader Service Dept.
P.O. Box 690, Rockville Centre, N.Y. 11571

Please send me the book(s) I have checked above. I am enclosi__
$_____ (please add $1.00 to cover postage and handlin__
Send check or money order only—no cash or C.O.D.'s.

Mr./Mrs./Miss _____

Address _____

City _____ State/Zip _____

Please allow six weeks for delivery. Prices subject to change with__